The CULLEN books by Mark Farrer (in chronological order):

Dirty Barry

Where Seagulls Dare

Bronchial Billy

A Fistful Of Collars

Pale Ale Rider

The Good The Bad & The Rugby

PALE ALE RIDER

mark farrer

funny business press

PALE ALE RIDER

ISBN: 978-1-9164892-6-4
Published by Funny Business Press

To the soup
For being so trustworthy.

This is a work of fiction.
Names, characters, places and incidents either are products of the author's imagination or are used fictitiously.
Any resemblance to actual events or locales or persons, living or dead, is entirely coincidental.
Except for Big Paul.

CONTENTS

ONE

Tyler McKenna was a complete bastard. Complete in the sense that he didn't want for anything. Because if he wanted something, he took it.

And he was a bastard in the literal sense of the word: born out of wedlock; illegitimate. His mother, Angela, had fallen pregnant while still at school and his father, Iain, had legged it before the birth and never been seen again. Well, almost never seen again - he was later spotted on Crimewatch.

The way Tyler saw it, his future had been predetermined. Raised on a sprawling estate, guns everywhere, one parent mostly absent, his father from a dysfunctional family with a long history of joblessness. An insightful observer could have pointed out that the same could be said for Prince Harry and he'd turned out alright - but there weren't many insightful observers in Tyler's orbit.

But despite this - or more correctly, perhaps, because of it - Tyler never had a problem coming into money. Usually because the money he came into was other peoples'. At school he had effortlessly acquired the dinner and pocket money of other children through ransacking of coats in cloakrooms, lockers in corridors, bags in changing rooms. Outside school, the money he acquired was his mother's. Dipping into her purse, nicking the odd quid here, a spare fiver there. She never noticed, or if she did she never said anything. Angela had an air of permanent exhaustion about her, a constant harried look - no doubt due to the fact that she held down two jobs to make ends meet. Not that this was in any way acknowledged or appreciated by her son - her absence at work, and the resulting lack of time spent with him, was just seen as further illustration of the parental neglect which had made him the way he was.

Even his mother's loving attempts to spend time with him went largely unappreciated. One of her jobs was at the Brewery and, from an early age, she had taken Tyler to work there - first as a kind of free creche and childcare facility where the other women on reception could coo and cuddle while she expressed milk; later, when she had taken on the job of delivery driver, she would let Tyler ride along in the cab with her during school holidays. What she might have considered entertainment, even education into the world of work, was certainly not what Tyler would call quality time. It was a chore, a drag and time spent away from his primary occupation: theft. An occupation which Tyler pursued smoothly and efficiently.

Because Tyler was smart and sly, and had no lack of planning or attention to detail. He would never take money where it would be unambiguously noticed - one pound coin from a purse containing several; just enough from a kid's coat to make them think they might have dropped some; graduating onto a few tenners from the Brewery Shop till loaded with them (never a twenty, or the highest denomination in the till). There was a permanent air of plausible deniability about any disappearance when Tyler was around - maybe it was him, maybe it wasn't. Or maybe there hadn't been any loss in the first place? Were you sure?

And it wasn't just cash. Tyler, like the taxman, was never happy. If someone had what he considered to be "too much" (and the strict definition of this term amounted, really, to "more than him") he had a roving eye and creative imagination.

When Tyler was six, his friend Joe (who had parents wealthy enough to afford two cars and a double garage to put them in) had put his hand in a garage door and then the door had slammed shut - in the wind, it seemed. Joe lost two fingers.

When he was eight, his next-door neighbour had three beautiful pedigree dachshunds which she was devoted to. Tyler had released four bars of Green's Organic Dark Chocolate from her kitchen cupboard onto the floor, testing out whether dogs could survive eating chocolate. They did - just. But shat all over an expensive Turkish rug and vomitted across a brand new sofa which never olfactorily recovered.

And later, at the Brewery, one full crate of beer amongst fifteen or so might cause Freddie doing the stock take to scratch his head and correct last week's figures. Tyler would never take one if there was a round number or an even, regular stack - but if there was a pile, he was in gravy.

No-one had a good word to say for Tyler, not that Tyler gave a toss. No-one, except for his mother. Angela wouldn't hear a bad word said about her beautiful baby boy - a child she doted on and had dedicated her life to raising and loving. Any criticism, accusation or negative feedback she heard about her son simply could not penetrate this confident forcefield of devotion. Were they sure? Everyone makes mistakes. Surely they were mistaken? Not her Tyler.

Like a weary pensioner with cataracts, Angela didn't so much navigate by what she saw as by the memory of what it had been last time she'd seen clearly. However long ago that was, probably the last time she'd had any energy to spare.

So Tyler slid through childhood and puberty like a shark, threatening but largely unobserved, and never in the vicinity when the damage was discovered. He wasn't some muscled or unintelligent thug - he was slight, not even that tall, and didn't look particularly prepossessing and certainly not intimidating. As an infant, he'd had the resting face of an angel - a cherub with apple cheeks, large liquid eyes, and a dimple in his chin which grew when he started to blubber. The slightest little thing could reduce him to tears, as if Bambi's mother had just died.

As he grew, his youthful chubbiness transformed into wiry, gawky pubescence, but he kept the almost baby-faced innocence, the demeanour of a pleasant if underachieving youngster. He had a shock of short, dark hair atop a narrow face of soft pale cheeks and a once-freckled stub of a nose.

But catch his face, one time, out of the corner of your eye. Or keep an unwavering gaze on him when he was unaware you were looking, and his face would somehow slacken. His facial muscles would loosen, skin tone switch and his eyes darken and you were looking at a different face - that of an unfeeling, dead-eyed man-child who could snap and spit, wound or injure without the slightest remorse. Insolent, hooded eyes which looked through you and dared you to react. Waited. Incited. Hoped.

And if you did, you never did it again.

But look again, and it was just Tyler, gazing at you enquiringly: *What?*

Tyler had the eyes of a serial killer. Could, perhaps one day, even become one - if only he had the ambition.

Tracey Mulhearn had ambition. She was the youngest of four girls, the other three all much older than her. Four daughters to four different fathers: Tyra, Tiffany, Teri and Tracey. Her elder sisters had all but left home by the time she was ten and her mother figured that, having taught her first three kids how to grow up, the last one would somehow pick it up through a kind of sororial osmosis. Plus her mother had quickly tired of the whole parenting lark: birthing four kids was quite bad enough without having to care for them alone when their co-creators had all fucked off at the first whiff of a full nappy.

Tracey's mother had had a hard time holding onto anything: boyfriends, money, reality. So Tracey had lacked a lot growing up, but she did have mental and physical energy to spare - and had needed to find outlets for it before she literally exploded. School certainly didn't do it for her. Not that she wasn't bright - she was; but the whole dull and grinding system and structure of study, revision, testing, attainment - endlessly repeating. She wanted more. She wanted X-Factor and recording contracts and blogging millions and... everything. Or, at least, anything but this boring nothingness which her painful teenage existence in some rural backwater involved. Biggar wasn't all that bad, she rationalised, but it wasn't New York, or London. Not even Manchester or Leeds. It was a sleepy, provincial town huddling nervously between Scotland's industrious central belt and England's domineering call and, like the red ribbon on a tug-of-war rope between two teams both tired of the game but too stubborn to quit, it was pulled this way and that but over the years the overall effect was that it essentially didn't go anywhere at all.

And if she stayed there, neither would she.

Tracey wanted more. She wanted excitement and danger, thrill and exhilaration. She wanted the needle to move and to hell with it.

And that was how it started.

"Hey." Tyler had pulled his mouth to one side, partly to exhale the smoke away from the girl, partly because he thought it might look cool.

The girl in black looked sullen and quiet, but very pretty nonetheless. Her hair was bright orange and chopped cruelly short and uneven, as if she'd been attacked by an aggressive strimmer, and she had artfully daubed on makeup - the way young girls do - attempting to achieve a unique look whilst ending up as a clone of all the other punk rebels in Biggar (there being nothing so unifying as a rebellion against one thing to make you resemble each other).

She was thin, almost gaunt, with hollow cheeks and narrow lips but bright round eyes which sparkled and flashed emerald. When she laughed - a dirty cynical laugh which sounded cruel and harsh - she rocked her head back to reveal a translucent, delicate neck with a perfect pale clavicle, partly-concealed by a washed-out grey T-shirt. Over this she wore a short black puffer jacket, shiny with wear. A badge on one lapel said "Nuclear Power: Yes Please"; the other lapel badge said "Nuclear Power: No Thanks". Her drainpipe black jeans, stick-thin, came to an end above a pair of Doc Martens trimmed with neon green socks peeping out the top. From one ear dangled a crucifix on a long chain, a blood-red metallic Christ painted on its silver cross; the other ear was penetrated by a gleaming sword, its hilt sitting outside her eardrum, and from its tip beneath her lobe dripped a small solitary ruby.

She looked up from her phone at Tyler through her scuffed fringe and then looked back down at it again, unimpressed. "Hey yourself."

"You new?"

"No." She snorted. "Don't make a habit of turning up, is all. School sucks."

"Right." Tyler nodded. He offered his open pack of cigarettes. "Smoke?"

She looked up at him, down at the pack, then up at him again. "Sure."

He fiddled getting the lighter from his pocket while she bent over to shield from any breeze. "Get caught?"

"No!" She puffed out some smoke, pouting. The very idea seemed to offend her. "Been called in, is why."

She spoke with a kind of mid-Atlantic accent but there was something about her speech pattern, and the way she used certain phrases, that made Tyler think she might be American - or, at the very least, heavily influenced by American TV shows.

"Right."

They stood leaning against the school wall, out of sight from the Science block, smoking in silence. The girl seemed in no mood to talk, focussed on her phone.

"I'm Tyler." He offered, hopefully.

"I know."

He waited for her to elaborate but she didn't. "Do I know you?"

"Not yet." She said, bored, and then shoved her phone into a pocket and turned to face him. "Do you want to?"

"Want to what?"

"Know me."

"Yeah."

"Why?"

Tyler was flummoxed. She was asking him a direct question and that always annoyed him. He liked to remain cool and aloof - enigmatic is what he thought of himself - and you couldn't be enigmatic if someone asked you a clear question, point blank. At least, he couldn't see how you could. He had a choice: sulk, snap back or be honest. He quickly weighed up these options.

"You look kinda cool." He said, boyishly.

She smiled. More than a smile, it brought her face alive and almost lit up his own.

"Tracey." She shook her head, still smiling, and looked him in the eye. "Wanna fuck?"

They lay, spent, on the mattress in Tracey's room. Tyler blowing cigarette smoke up into the air, jiggling his jaw, trying to make smoke rings. He was desperate to impress her; aching to show her that he was a real man, older than his years, worldly-wise and someone to be admired. Not the young, adolescent scumbag that he actually was.

"How many times have you had sex?"

Tyler was instantly on his guard. He hadn't expected that he would need to conjure up an impressive sexual backstory. At least, not right now, having so recently done the deed for what - only the third time?

"Oh, loads." He shrugged, reckoning that, given the exact wording of her question, wanks should count.

"With how many girls?"

"Oh, we're just talking about girls are we?" Tyler

spontaneously threw this in and then immediately realised this might not play too well.

"What do you mean?" Her brow creased and she propped herself up on one elbow next to him to look into his eyes. Tyler panicked.

"Nothing. I'm only joking." He smiled apologetically, and his mind raced as he tried to find a way to answer her question without admitting his lack of sexual experience. On the one foreign school trip he had ever been on, he had got off with a girl from Rio de Janeiro who had been backpacking around Italy. He leapt at this recollection like a tramp on a ham & cheese toastie. "I've slept with a Brazilian!" Tyler boasted.

"OMFG!" Tracey shrieked in horror. "How many is a brazillion?"

They had settled on an M.O quickly and readily. Responsibilities divided naturally enough, since Tyler wanted to make sure everything went according to his meticulous plans, and didn't trust anyone else not to cock it up. And Tracey wanted to ride Tyler's bike.

For someone who had a motorbike, Tyler didn't seem to care much for it. It was almost as if he had got it because it was expected of him. A bike to make him look cool and hard and tough, but he didn't like it because it was noisy and fast and it freaked him out when he went round corners too fast.

And he hid it from his mother. How embarrassing was that? "She'd kill me if I had one!" he had almost whined, and Tracey had looked at him as if he had just admitted to watching Downton.

"Unlikely." Tracey had offered. "She's your mother."

"Well, ground me then."

"Ground you? What are you, ten?"

Tyler had sulked for a while after that. Until she had sucked his cock.

But he had a motorbike nonetheless and Tracey's eyes had lit up when she had seen it. He had stolen it from someone's backyard in Penicuik and it was neon orange and black, chrome and white and it shone and sparkled while he kept it clean and new. And it wasn't just the fact that he had stolen it which had added to its appeal - it was Tyler's approach to stuff which she found fascinating and strangely alluring. Partially because it was so alien to her: she was impulsive and wild - some would call her random and scatty; he was methodical and planned. He would construct a plan in his head, work out all the steps and then proceed to follow them one by one in order to achieve his goal.

Need a motorbike? Well, he couldn't buy one - he was still too young. And they would likely want to know where he'd got the money from. But he could steal one. But stealing a motorbike meant they'd be on the lookout for it, once it had been stolen. So you needed to steal it from somewhere far away - or at least far enough away so that it was in a different constabulary or county, somewhere the police who spotted you riding it wouldn't care too much about.

Biggar was in South Lanarkshire, near the western boundary with the Scottish Borders; Penicuik was in Midlothian, just beyond the northern boundary. The two towns were only twenty miles apart but not just in different counties, they were separated by a third. The long, smooth A702 was a smashing 30 minute thrill-ride from one to the other on a bike and it had been oh-so-simple for Tyler to catch a bus, scout out Penicuik, find a suitable target, steal himself some bolt-cutters and thus acquire a shiny new bike.

Tyler stashed it in The Cave, as he insisted on calling it. A large storage container which sat out back, behind the Brewery outbuildings, where the edge of the site met a largely unused paddock. The container had been abandoned and neglected for some years now, and so far Tyler had done nothing with it except use it to stash anything he had acquired that he wanted to hide from his mother.

Which was everything he had acquired. Including his bike.

Tracey loved the bike, and every chance she got to ride it. The feeling of power at her instant control, the way it reacted and moved with her, the slightest changes of balance allowing her to sway it, violently if need be, this way and that. It was like besting a wild animal with convenient domestic controls.

While Tyler was busy planning each job, she had busied herself buying accessories, riding attire and addressing herself to the interior decor of their, now shared, Cave. She had spent half a weekend mopping and cleaning it out before starting the process of turning it into a kind of teenage studio apartment. Tyler thought she was mad and looked at her with a disbelieving off-kilter squint, like a Scotsman being asked if he'd like another drink. She had blithely ridden out his indifference and later his ridicule, buying his-and-hers helmets *"What the fuck? Do you want us to get noticed?"*, matching leather jackets, *"How many places do we have to rob before we make this much back?"* and then moving onto soft furnishings and IKEA basics *"Make sure you pay cash. Avoiding traceability is key."*

Surprised, she had given herself a good talking to in case she was unknowingly overseeing a metamorphosis from hardened, rebellious wannabe rock-chick to mumsy-homemaker-in-waiting. Tracey reassured herself that, genetically, she didn't have it in her. This was simply the first time she had had anywhere she could call her own, the first time she had any money to speak of, and the first time she had *carte-blanche* to exercise some decision-making which resulted in actual material change. If their new *pied-a-terre* and all the *accoutrements* that went with it (Tracey idly wondered if perhaps she wasn't half-French) was a life of crime, Tracey loved it and wanted more of it. She would urge Tyler on with greater urgency, using her sex and her ideas to entice, persuade and upgrade Tyler's own self-limiting ambitions.

As for the M.O., Tracey had gazed longingly at his bike while Tyler had explained, at length, the why's and wherefore's behind his thinking.

During school holidays, he had ridden in his mother's delivery van every day as she made her deliveries for the Brewery. They would pull up at a pub, the time and date unvarying: each pub had a set delivery day of the week, and his mother always did the round in the same order so the times were reliable, traffic and weather permitting.

At first Tyler would wait in the cab, idling on his phone and listening to some frantic *um-tsch-um-tsch-um-tsch* in his earbuds while his mother usually walked through a rear access door, always open, docket in hand and would return a minute or so later with a member of staff who would help unload the kegs and crates. Occasionally he would be called on to help, perhaps hold a door open or move some empties to one side to allow better access to the cellar or storeroom. But over the weeks Tyler had started taking more of an interest in things.

There was always, *always*, a back door open. Sometimes it was to vent heat or let in some fresh air, sometimes it was so that the kitchen staff could pop outside for a smoke, sometimes it was to allow easy access for rubbish to be piled by the door for collection. Whatever the reason, there was always an open back door to each pub premises and it was only manned when some stray employee sneaked out for a quick drag.

All Tyler had to do was walk in. So, one day, he did. And the following week. And the week after that. Over the course of one summer holiday he walked into a dozen different pubs and clubs, each time venturing further into the dark corridors and empty rooms, kitchens or offices, wandering around until he found something of value. It could have been a till, or a safe, or a trophy cabinet. Whatever it was, Tyler made a mental note and had later drawn up a detailed sketch of the layout, location of important items, doorways, likely position of staff, etc.

During each of the forays he was always ready to stumble upon someone who would ask who he was and what he was doing there, and he had an answer ready which was *"My Mum's delivering beer from the Brewery and I needed a wee."* Which, he thought, would be fair enough and indeed, one time he had been startled to turn a corner and find two kitchen employees trying to wrestle each other's tongues out of their heads. They had jumped, he had jumped, extended his story and ended up in the lavatories, gaining access to more of the building's interior en route. Thereafter, he was quite hoping to be discovered as it would aid his study of each place.

He soon had schematics and details of these separate establishments and started trial runs - small stuff at first.

Stuff he could put into his pockets and return to his mother's cab with, undetected and unsuspected. By the end of the summer holidays he had an intimate knowledge of these twelve places, and a small treasure trove of stolen items ranging from expensive-looking kitchen knives, through some very smart pairs of workboots, to the contents of three separate petty cash boxes.

He felt like a Master of the Universe, able to come and go at will - the Macavity of Pub crimes. Never seen, never suspected, never caught. Now, the pair of them together could move on up the value chain and find something better to steal.

"What do you say, Trace?"

"Hmm? Yeah. Cool." Tracey tore her eyes from the beautiful bike and tried to zone back into whatever Tyler had been saying. "What's our next target then?"

"I just told you. The Lamb & Flag."

"Right. Yeah. Gotcha. Just checking. Yeah."

From the get-go, Tracey had seen Tyler and his methodical planning as the hallmarks of a criminal mastermind. His ability to think through situations, predict outcomes and allow for things going wrong. It was some kind of magic, watching him think and then listening to him outline the plan in glorious shining detail.

But perhaps, Tracey was starting to wonder, he was methodical to the extent of being predictable and boring. And while Tyler could be relied upon to plan, work out the details and the order of events and follow it through, he was easily derailed by the unexpected. It was as if he had to have time to assess whatever it was, process it, work out a series of responses, select the right one and then put it into action. This all took time. It was like watching an AI computer responding in slow-mo. He seemed to have no instincts, no ability to function on autopilot without having been pre-programmed. You could never picture him, for example, catching a ball. The time taken to inform him a ball was on its way, locate its position in the air, identify its trajectory, plot its final catchable position, work out how to arrange his body to be in the right place at the right time and in the right arrangement of arms, legs, weight distribution and hand placement... the ball would just hit him in the face.

No, with Tyler you needed to pre-announce well in advance, provide all the parameters and address all of his concerns. Once done, you could rely on him to be there and carry out all the necessary steps to complete the task. All the eventualities he had foreseen, all the mistakes that could happen, he would be prepared for. But if something unanticipated went wrong, you were fucked.

And things were starting to go wrong. A lot.

They'd hit three pubs and one Ex-servicemen's club and the returns had been less than glorious. In fact, they had nearly been caught at the club when a different delivery lorry had turned up at the same time and blocked Tracey's exit route. Tyler had come whizzing out of the side door, pulled up sharply to avoid the reversing lorry, cashbox flying open and spewing its contents everywhere. She had had to manually jiggle and hump the bike through the narrowest of gaps between the lorry and the wall, while the unwitting driver shouted at them to get out of the way. She had fishtailed down the road, Tyler clinging on for dear life, her own pulse pounding in her temple.

Learning curve, Tyler called it. Bollocks, more like.

So while Tracey relished to some extent the danger and

risk that these adrenalin-filled cock-ups provided, she was also concerned that while they represented to Tyler opportunities for improvement, honing the plan and building a more robust process, to her they represented an increasing probability of being caught.

And that wasn't in her plans, thank you very much.

But she knew that Tyler wouldn't just let her go if she left, wouldn't accept it as some kind of clean, sudden break. He'd be clingy, she bet. Whiny. Tyler was like a minefield: easy to lay, a nightmare to get rid of. He would beg for a second chance or become some kind of stalker. That was what she was afraid of - she really didn't like the thought of some black-eyed proto-killer creeping around after her, seeking reconciliation and, when that didn't materialise, revenge.

She needed a dumping strategy. Some kind of unequivocal descent of their relationship such that the final kiss-off would be clean and inevitable. Like knocking over a coke machine - you didn't do it all in one go. You had to rock it back and forwards a few times. Build momentum.

TWO

The first thing Paul saw when he turned back to the waiting kegs was his reflection in the mirrored visor. The second thing he saw was the knife gleam as the figure in the black motorcycle helmet raised his left arm in this shadowed section of the cellar.

Instinctively, Paul dipped his right shoulder away so that any swing from his attacker would put him out of knife range. It was a large chef's knife, sharp as hell by the look of it and, if it had been swiped from the kitchen in The Lamb & Flag, Paul knew it would be razor keen - through lack of use. Davy's kitchen output would never be mistaken for *haute cuisine* and microwaving frozen stuff didn't require much in the way of knife skills from what passed as his kitchen staff. Not that Paul could criticise - his personal culinary repertoire ran a limited gamut from *Saucisson en croute avec sauce brun* to *Digits de poisson et sauce rouge*. He may not have known one end of a mandolin from another but, in his capacity as experienced joiner and cabinetmaker, he was well versed in handling tools which could inflict serious damage. He knew a dangerous knife when he saw one.

The pair stood frozen, spotlit by the shaft of bright daylight streaming down into the beer cellar through the open hatch above. Paul raised both hands and swivelled his eyes this way and that for any kind of assistance or exit strategy. Through the hatchway came the sound of Davy humping a barrel onto the van and shouting down for the next one.

"Come on, Beep!" Davy's disembodied cry rang down in the echoing cellar. "On the clock here. Let's be having you."

His attacker glanced up, startled at the sound of another voice, and Paul seized his chance. He grabbed the empty keg nearest his right hand and swung it round in front of him, just as the helmeted figure slashed in his direction. The knife glanced off the metal barrel with a clang and clattered to the floor. The biker, now unarmed, started to back away, the helmet now scanning left and right for the nearest exit. Paul hefted the keg easily in his giant grasp and launched it straight at his attacker. The slender figure took this solid weight full in the chest and fell backwards onto the concrete floor as the remaining momentum of the metal cylinder sent it rolling noisily to a stop in the shadows.

Paul stood, unsure to what to do next, as the figure scrambled quickly but shakily to his feet, took one last look at Paul and then fled through the swing doors into the kitchen corridor. Whilst Paul hadn't been able to see a bloody thing through that visor, he was nevertheless convinced that the masked figure had glared at him, squinting menace in his eyes, as if to say *I'll be back.*

It was now that Paul realised he had been holding his breath this whole time and he exhaled in a heavy stream and bent down, meaty palms resting on his thighs. He heard a sudden commotion coming from the kitchen and froze again, only to recognise the clatter and growl of the landlord as he hustled down the narrow space between the stainless steel countertops and out into the corridor which led to the cellar. The sweating, red face of an annoyed

Davy appeared through the swingdoors, barking at anyone within earshot which, right now, was only Paul.

"Ere! Who's had my best knife?"

So this was it. This was the official beginning of the end. The coke machine was on the move.

Tyler had come half-running, half-limping round the corner screaming at her through his motorcycle helmet - she couldn't make out a fucking word he was saying, but there was clear and definite urgency in his tone. Tracey had revved the engine and zoomed off almost before he had settled on the pillion behind her. The bike had lurched forward, threatening to wheelie alarmingly with the extra weight and her over-enthusiastic revving, and they had careered down the road with Tyler hanging onto her with one hand and banging her side with the other in a gesture she later found meant slowdown but, at the time, she had taken to mean speed up.

They had rowed as soon as they were safely out of town and tucked away up a dirt track in the forest. Tracey had pulled up at a passing place and turned off the ignition. Amid the summer heat, the woods suddenly felt cool and silent.

"What the fuck did you do that for?" Tyler had taken off his helmet, his hair dripping and plastered to his head, sweat from adrenalin, tension, fear. There were stains under his armpits and his T-shirt was sticking to his back as he pulled himself off the bike.

"Do what for?"

"Shoot off before I was safely on the back? I nearly fell off!"

"You came pelting out of the pub, bellowing and

waving your arms in the air. I took that to mean you needed a speedy getaway." Tracey leant forwards at the waist, hands on her hips, leaning into the argument in case she needed extra emphasis.

"Yeah, well I did. But I wanted to come away alive."

"Well." She splayed out both arms. "Here we are!"

Tyler harrumphed and contorted himself trying to wipe his sweaty head on the capped sleeves of his T-shirt.

"So. What did you get?" Tracey asked.

"My head caved in. Nearly." He sighed heavily and looked at her with his brow creased. She couldn't work out if he was annoyed, worried or both.

"And... the money?"

"No."

"What? Why not?"

"I took a wrong turn and ended up in the cellar in front of some big lump. He threw a keg at me and I legged it." Tyler looked suddenly rather pale.

"My hero."

"Well, what the fuck would you have done, hmm? Bloke was the size of a tanker and I was off-guard."

"The landlord?"

"No. The landlord's a wheezy, weedy guy. This bloke was big." He suddenly twisted away from her, and threw up over a stand of tulips growing by the side of the track. It wasn't annoyance or worry, she realised.

"You total chicken." She spat the words, amplifying her disdain.

"What?"

"You pathetic, cowardly little shit."

"Fuck you, Trace." Tyler wheeled round and his eyes flared black and bright, all evidence of fear now vanished. Tracey hesitated for an instant, suddenly scared, but stood her ground.

"Fuck me? No chance. I don't sleep with little girls." She sneered. Tyler glared at her but said nothing. *"He threw a keg at me and I legged it."* She piped in a toddler voice, mincing as she did so. "Pathetic."

"Yeah? Well what would you have done, huh?"

"I don't know. Maybe, you know, like... fight?"

"He was big."

"So? Was he armed?"

"No."

"Were you?"

"No." Tyler said, reddening.

"You fucking liar!" Tracey's eyes widened and her disgust pounced on her receding fear and beat it to a pulp. She moved in on Tyler, real pity on her face. "You were armed! And you fucking ran?"

"He threw a keg at me!" Tyler whined. "The knife fell-"

"You had a knife!"

"He had a keg."

"He had a keg." She mimicked again.

"What could I have done, hmm?"

"Ooh, I don't know. Maybe you could have thrown up on him."

"Ha fucking ha."

"It's not funny, Ty. It is seriously not funny." Tracey shook her head, half in sadness and half in recognition.

"Am I laughing? No." Tyler looked at her intently but she had lost interest.

"Me neither."

"Look." Tyler grabbed her by the shoulders, trying to get her to look at him. "What do we do? We go back. We hit them again. And if he's there again... I shank him!"

"You shank him?" She looked up all right. And laughed in his face.

"I shank him." Tyler insisted, his face steely. "You in?"

"No."

"What? Why not?"

"Something's come up."

"What?"

My standards, Tracey thought. But she just shook her head and said nothing.

Cullen sometimes felt as if he had been born to walk. Trails, woods, fields, hills - the simple act of putting one foot in front of the other gave him serenity and calm. Others chose meditation or yoga, knitted or did crosswords. Cullen walked. It helped slot his crowded thoughts snugly into place and brought perspective and order to his troubled mind. He could feel the cool air on his face, or the patter of rain on his faithful hat, as the steady drip of the miles and the hours passed beneath his battered boots. They'd need replacing soon.

So, perhaps, would his hips. It had been a long time, wandering. Searching but never finding, only the journey keeping him sane.

Over the years he had wandered, his path stretching across the country, spanning East and West, descending down to the very border with England and as far North as Nairn - where his wife had been born. Scotland offered immense beauty and intense landscapes: cold granite faces, stone crags softened with moss, heathered hillsides and boggy moorlands, deep green coniferous swathes hovering over lochs of cold, liquid slate. The air, the sky, were ever changing - the wind could carry signs of welcome or danger, smells of hearth or damp, sounds of beauty or fear. For those who knew where to look, and what to look for.

Cullen had learned this, and more, as he had walked. And across those years, whenever he could, he had sought out shelter amongst the trees. Woods, forests, glades, copses. They hid you, gave you warmth, provided resources and security. The smell of pine needles laid soft and thick beneath the trees, the way the sound of the air was deadened and hushed by the branches, the wind marshalled and subdued, the slightest movement or change amplified and instantly detected. These forests of fir were his preference - his sanctuary - and he sought out their density whenever he could.

He had been hiking for days, slowly and systemically - he was getting slower these days, he knew, and he wasn't at all happy about it. But his route had been methodical, even if it wouldn't have appeared so on any map. Methodical and reasoned, retracing old steps, re-examining long-forgotten thoughts, seeking an epiphany amidst the past. He had come up along the Annandale Way, passing through Lochmaben, onto Moffat, traversing the Devil's Beef Tub before crossing to the Southern Upland Way and heading northeast towards the forests around Traquair. Here he had changed direction again, almost doubling back and heading due west across the hills between Peebles and Stobo, and onto Drumelzier and Broughton. The miles had stolen his hours and his thoughts, his footsteps leading him trance-like over the hills.

Which is how he reached the former railway line, long dismantled, which led to Biggar, its abandoned path running unkempt and neglected alongside Biggar Water and the small brewery which nestled there. There was no tree cover here, no lee where contours hid you from sight. It was a late June afternoon, the sun had been warm and constant, it was a further flat five miles into town and the smell of brewing had hit him like an alien, acrid fist - an unwelcome assault which made him realise how dog-tired he was. He was dead on his feet, his feet had known it for a while, and Cullen reluctantly gave in to their demands.

The small footbridge over the burn brought him up right onto the brewery premises, outbuildings and trailers littering a large flat asphalt square which was fed by a tarmac ribbon to the main road. Behind the main buildings, amidst what there was around here passing for foliage and cover, was an old storage container - a dulled burgundy lego brick, edged and brushed with low trees and bushes. Cullen didn't pause to reconsider, he instinctively knew there was no-one around and he stole the moment while he had it. Reaching the container across the clear area of tarmac took less than thirty seconds and, once there, he was able to duck behind the far side, between the bushes and its warm metal wall, and sit down in the shade.

He nodded off and when he awoke he was initially confused to find himself staring at nettles and brambles close up. He picked a few blackberries and chewed them, their dark sweetness flooding his mouth and he realised he was thirsty and out of water. With a new sense of urgency, he pushed himself back to his feet and ventured around the side of the container to the back doors. All was quiet and still now around the brewery and the sun had a welcome evening warmth to it, but the back of the container was locked.

This rear-end of the storage unit entirely comprised

two double doors, held in place by four vertical rods which slotted into metal housings top and bottom. The horizontal levers which swivelled the housings open were secured inside a covered lockbox in the centre where the door panels met. Accessible only from beneath, this metal lockbox contained a heavy-duty padlock, shiny and new - unlike the steel rods and levers on the doors, which were weathered and rusted in places.

Cullen pondered for a moment, weighing up the different courses of action open to him, and then reached into his pack for his set of lock picks, the barest smile of resignation playing across his lips.

Twenty minutes later, what little humour he retained had evaporated and the padlock remained stubbornly oblivious. Maybe it was some new type of lock, more difficult to crack? But whilst it was clearly new there was nothing about it that said expensive or premium. It looked like any other bog standard padlock. That left the possibilities that he was out of practice or losing his touch. Or just plain bloody exhausted, he accepted. Irritated now, he manhandled his tools more roughly and felt the sweatband in his hat overloading, the salt trickles pooling in his eyebrows. His vision swam and then doubled as he tried, and failed, to make progress. The air grew muggy and he found himself wheezing, the effort in breathing making his ribs hurt.

He looked at his watch, realising he couldn't quite make out what time it was, and came wearily to a decision. Scrabbling back out of sight, he leant against the side of the sun-warmed container, and slid down onto the dry ground. With the heat of the ridged metal oozing into his back, Cullen pulled his hat down over his eyes and let sleep take him.

"Where's the rest?" Carl looked askance at the single crate of beer in the middle of the floor, then scouted around the echoing container - unfruitfully. A forty foot-long, all-metal box with no windows, the recent warm spell meant a furnace-blast sirocco flew out at you whenever you unlocked the rear doors - like a curse escaping Tutenkhamen's tomb. The only ventilation available when the doors were closed were a series of small vents set in regular intervals high up in the sidewalls. Not enough to make the container unseaworthy, just sufficient to allow a trickle of air in and out, so if you spent an hour sitting inside you emerged blinking, sweating and gulping for air like some exhausted turtle dragging itself up the beach after swimming the Atlantic.

Propped up against the bare left wall was a set of low chipboard shelves piled with cardboard boxes, some open. Inside one was a set of sweatshirts, still tagged and in polythene. Further down was an old mahogany wardrobe, locked, which also acted as some kind of room divider and behind it were two stacks of beer crates, some containing unopened bottles, and a pile of empties on the floor beside them. Over in the corner was an inflatable double mattress on top of a large rug, pillows and a uncovered duvet thrown casually across it. An open suitcase lay on the floor beside this bed, unfolded clothes topped with scattered make-up, toiletries and a hairbrush.

The right-hand side of this sectioned-off bedroom was a head-high wall of more boxes, all still sealed, forming a smaller enclosure. Inside this were more beer crates, empty this time, topped with a door acting as a rudimentary worksurface. This was littered with empty fastfood cartons, pizza boxes and opened tins of beans. A two-litre bottle of Irn-Bru brooded half-full over proceedings. Leaning against this set of boxes was a motorbike, with glistening chrome wheels and bright orange petrol tank, the grain on the black leather seats catching whatever light was played on it.

This was The Cave: Tyler and Tracey's home from home, their secret hideout. Out in the wider world they were Tyler and Tracey; here they were forging a new identity and living it out. Here they were Bonnie & Clyde. And Carl - when he turned up.

"'S all there is." Tyler grunted. "Stop your fucking complaining. It's free isn't it?"

"I'm not complaining, Ty." Carl backed off, palms up, at the flash in Tyler's eyes.

"Sounds like you are." Tyler's snarled. "It's fucking free is what it is. And you should be grateful. Don't see you ever bringing anything to the party."

"Don't have your gift, do I?" Carl said, a compliant half-smile on his face. Carl knew better than to rile his friend, knew his place in the order of things and, truth be told, was happy to not be top dog. Top dog meant getting into fights, putting your neck on the line, being a rebel. Carl wasn't big on rebellion. Rebellion for Carl was putting the immersion heater on when his parents went out. No, he was happy to be the tagalong helpmeet, combined bigger-upper and dogsbody. Duties: do as you're told, take jokes like a man, and sit back and benefit from the bounty that the top dog brought to the table.

He was a little taller than Tyler, with a head of shaggy blonde hair and a Roman nose proudly situated between two innocent blue-green eyes. All of which made him look like he'd been to a posh public school and smelled fantastic, though neither were the case. He was a little bit chunkier than Tyler and a little bit slower on the uptake and had somehow been sucked up in Tyler's vortex at High School and carried along like a confused cow in a tornado. That had been some time ago now, but each seemed to appreciate the other for reasons neither could fully understand, so the status quo had generally and smoothly persisted.

"This'll do me anyway!" Carl cheered, elbowing Tracey in the ribs. "What're the rest of you having?"

"I told you." Tyler growled. "This is ALL there is."

"Only joking, Ty." Carl smiled broadly in an attempt at mollification.

"Plus the emergency backup!" Tracey announced, coming out from behind the wardrobe with another full crate.

"Yay!" Carl rubbed his hands. "Game on."

"Forgotten we had that." Tyler nodded to Tracey, pleasantly surprised.

"Right, what have you got?" Said Carl, rubbing his hands.

"Let's see... we have *Hop To It, Don't Worry Be Hoppy, Hop Replacement Therapy* and... *Barley's Ghost.*"

"Barley's Ghost?" Carl wrinkled his nose, brow furrowed. "I don't get it."

"Hmm. Me neither." Tracey admitted, giving a thoughtful little moue.

"It's Dickens." Tyler sighed. "Marley's Ghost. A Christmas Carol?" He looked disappointed at the blank faces around him. "Scrooge?"

"Oh, Scrooge! Got it, yeah." Carl lied, smoothly flipping off the bottle cap and taking a sniff. "Smells like... beer!"

"As opposed to?"

"Just sayin'." Carl looked at the label. "A smooth, caramel-flavoured ale with dark-roasted malted barley and our own special hops to give a unique Christmassy feel!"

"In June." Tyler's lip curled.

"Hmmm." Carl took a sip and smiled. "Well, beauty is in the eye of the beer holder."

"Just drink it, would you?" Tyler ordered.

"Yessir!" Carl happily obliged. "And if someone asks why I'm drinking beer this early in the day I can say I was only obeying orders!" He saluted playfully and then necked the bottle.

"I'll have a Hop Replacement Therapy." Tyler nodded to Tracey who passed him a bottle over.

"Why do they all have punny names then, these beers?" Carl wondered aloud, placing his empty gently on the floor

"It's a thing." Tyler said.

"I can see that. Beer me!" Carl shouted to Tracey.

"The brewery likes it. Makes their stuff more distinctive."

"Huh." Carl nodded and broke the top off another bottle.

"I heard the Marketing Director talking about brand names the other day."

"Ooh, get you! Marketing Director, is it?"

"It's his job title." Tyler sneered. "Not mine."

"Right." Carl acknowledged. "Soz."

"There was some kind of argument about the name for a new beer. This marketing guy was having a strop."

"Strop? Is that a Czech beer?"

"Carl." Tyler glared. "Fuck. Off."

"Ok, ok." Carl sighed. "Funny's off the menu today is it? I get it."

"Funny is off the menu, yes. And the reason it is off the menu is because we nearly got caught."

"Again." Chimed in Tracey. Tyler glared at her and she cracked a weak smile.

"And it is also off the menu because we only have one crate left."

"Two!" Tracey chimed in, pointing at the emergency crate.

"Two." Tyler turned his head, slowly, towards Tracey and she obediently drew a line across her lips with her thumb and forefinger.

"Well, get some more then. Simples!" Carl shrugged, his eyebrows communicating the genius of his idea while he chugged on his beer.

"Simple is it?" Tyler stepped menacingly towards his friend. "And what about the security cameras, hmm?"

"What cameras?" Carl started to retreat, worry on his face.

"The fucking cameras they're putting in tomorrow next door, dickbrain. Do you want me to get caught?"

"Why are they putting cameras in?"

"Because someone has been stealing money and beer from the brewery." Tyler's sneer could not have been more withering.

"They're onto you!" Carl blurted.

"No. They are not."

"And you nearly got caught!"

"No. We did not." Tyler glared at Tracey willing her to contradict him. She held his gaze for a second before looking away.

"The net is closing in!"

"Will you stop squealing like a fucking baby." Tyler's face was now thrust right up into Carl's, his friend pinned against the wall of boxes.

"He's right, Ty." Tracey spoke up softly.

"No, he's fucking not!" Tyler spat, his glare switching from Carl to Tracey and back again.

"Maybe we should stop for a while?" She offered.

"Stop?" Tyler turned away from Carl and moved to the middle of the floor. "Stop? Are you scared?"

"Yeah, Trace." Carl curled his lip, his sympathies latching back onto his friend now that there was some physical distance between them once more. "Think about the beer. If you won't do it for yourself, at least do it for the beer!"

"I'm not scared." Tracey returned, defiant.

"Good. So, the cameras rule out the brewery? Fine. Doesn't mean we can't carry on with the pubs and clubs."

"Hear, hear!" Carl raised his bottle in sozzled salute.

"And I'm not standing for it." Tyler started to pace, weighing his own bottle in his hand. "I've told Trace - we're having a piece of that Lamb & Flag. If that fucking fat bastard thinks he can deny me, he's got another think coming."

"Hurray!" Carl said and then stopped suddenly, cocking his head to one side. "Did you hear something?"

"No." Tyler looked across at Tracey who shook her head.

"Listen." Carl shhh'ed them and they all listened for a moment.

Tyler peered out through the daylight crack between the open doors of the container and saw nothing, but his hackles rose nonetheless. "Carl? Go check."

Carl, recognising the time had come for him to do his share, dutifully rose. "Here, hold my beer." And he stepped out into the hazy evening heat.

Carl blinked hard to try and adjust to the bright daylight after the darkness of the stuffy container. He felt the warm breeze on his skin wicking away some of the sweat it had acquired and curled his head slightly at the pleasant sensation, like a cat being stroked. He peered down the side of the container and saw only a mash of brambles, nettles and bushes which dwindled to a stop at the edge of the concrete hardpad on which the storage unit stood. A few empty bottles, carrier bags and cans lay scattered along the foot of the high container walls.

"Anything?" Tyler's voice came from inside.

"No." Carl stage-whispered over his shoulder.

"Go round!" Came the hiss.

Carl listened, heard nothing, and started padding slowly down the side of the unit. As he neared the corner he heard a loud clink of bottles and stopped, his lead foot mid-air. He swallowed hard and realised he had no weapon on him. Torn between the possible danger ahead and the certain wrath of Tyler behind if he didn't complete his task, he took a deep breath and poked his head around the side of the container.

He saw the back a lime green waterproof coat disappear around the other corner, clinking through a large pile of discarded beer bottles as it did so. Carl sprang forward and shot towards the vacated corner. When he turned it, he saw Tyler facing him at the far end of the container, partially obscured by the figure in lime green. He was several inches taller and broader than Tyler and was wearing a battered leather cowboy hat.

"Who the fuck are you?" Tyler's face had slackened, his eyes hooded and black. He didn't seem at all concerned about the size difference between himself and this stranger.

"I'm me." The man spoke, his voice quiet but steady. Although Carl could only see his back, the stranger didn't seem particularly worried or concerned about being threatened in this way. "Who're you?"

Carl's eyes widened as he saw Tyler heft the beer bottle into his left hand so that he was holding it by the neck, the last dregs dribbling onto the ground, and smash it against the side of the trailer. Glass shards and splinters glittered in the light as they fell onto the grass and an evil smile played across Tyler's lips.

"Let me introduce myself. I'm the bad guy."

It might not be much right now, but Tyler was proud of this place and his booty. He might owe the decorative touches to Tracey but the contents of The Cave - the beer, the boxes, the bike - that was all his. His idea, his efforts, his reward. And if this fucking cowboy thought he was going to nick it, or dob them all in, he was very much mistaken. Tyler didn't know if this man had overheard them talking, but he wasn't about to take any chances. He held his beer bottle threateningly by the neck and glared at the intruder, daring him to respond or react.

Annoyingly the man did neither. He just stood there, silently, his eyes alert and his stance open, both hands palms-facing, spread to either side, his feet apart as if ready to bear his weight for a long time.

The man was tall, around six foot, Tyler reckoned, maybe more. It was difficult to tell with the stupid cowboy hat he was wearing. Taller than himself anyway, and whilst he wasn't bulky he looked athletic and fit. His eyes were grey, almost faded beneath the shade of his grizzled eyebrows, and his face was lined and weatherbeaten - the face of a man jaded by experience and disappointment. There were no laughter lines, no trace of a smile. This face spoke of sadness, resilience and steel. And he seemed not at all perturbed that Tyler was holding a jagged bottle on him. But Tyler was small and wiry, a whippet to this man's scruffy Irish setter. He could bite and he wasn't afraid to attack. He just wasn't sure whether this man cared.

"Talk, fucker." Tyler shoved his beer bottle front and centre, rising onto the balls of his feet. The man didn't move.

"Hello."

"What?" Tyler snorted.

"Hello." The man repeated, his voice quiet but distinct. Tyler frowned, disconcerted further.

"Hello? Fucking Hello? What the fuck is this? What the fuck are you doing here?"

"Looking for a place to sleep." A simple statement of fact. Tyler didn't like this at all. Tracey appeared behind him, suddenly interested, and pulled playfully on a string of her chewing gum.

"Well, tough shit, Granddad. This place is taken."

"I can see that."

The man remained motionless and Tyler turned to look at Tracey, as if to say, *You getting this? Is this guy for real?* Tracey draped an arm over Tyler's shoulder - part assurance, part decoration. She looked amusingly at the man in the hat.

"Cut him, Ty. Cut him." She purred into his ear, and Tyler felt himself getting hard at the thought of taking a slice out of this stranger and then celebrating with Tracey on the mattress in The Cave, a slick of his blood on the floor nearby.

Tyler smiled. "You just barged into the wrong place, Granddad."

"Well, in that case. I suppose I will be going." The man pulled one side of his mouth tight, in a sort of half-smile, eyes on the bottle, but kept both hands out at his sides.

"Oh, not now, Granddad. Too late now. You've heard too much."

"What have I heard?" The man raised his eyebrows. "Some kids having fun in an abandoned storage container?"

"You say that now."

"What else would I say? And who would I say it to?"

"You're not going to say anything. To anyone." Tyler smiled, mock-apologetically, and shrugged his shoulders. "You need something to remind you to keep your mouth shut, I reckon."

"Do I? You have a choice. There's always a choice."

"Choice? No choices here, Granddad." Tyler cocked his head as Tracey whispered in his ear. He switched his attention back to the man, a slick grin on his sneering face. The man looked down at the ground, seemingly lost in thought for a moment, and then looked up and held Tyler's stare.

"Do I know you?"

"I... don't think so." The question threw Tyler momentarily and he blinked, confused, then recovered his composure. "I think you'd remember me. Don't you?"

"Definitely."

Tyler screwed up his face into a ball of hate. "Fuck this. We're done here. You're done here." Tracey withdrew from his shoulder and Tyler lunged forwards, and in one smooth move found himself disarmed and folded up in pain on the grass, clutching his elbow. Somehow the man had side-stepped his thrust, grabbed his wrist and cracked his arm over his knee. The bottle had dropped into the nettles and Tyler's elbow throbbed like it had been removed, hit with a lump hammer, and then put on backwards.

Tracey's mouth fell open, gum-chewing momentarily suspended.

The man stooped slowly to pick up his hat which had fallen off in the brief attack, adjusted it carefully on his head and then strode calmly towards the corner of the container and the paddock beyond. Carl and Tracey watched him leave. Tyler still lay writhing on the ground, trying not to cry out.

The man paused briefly, peering in through the open rear doors to The Cave. "Nice bike." He said, and then was gone.

THREE

"Chuffing bastard." Muttered Freddie, as soon as he was out of Arthur's earshot. He had avoided slamming the office door, but only just. He paced up and down the warehouse corridor, like a man who couldn't find his haemorrhoid cream: annoyed and pained in equal measure.

His loyalty to the brewery had once again got the better of his anger and frustration. That and Arthur's calm diplomacy and just-bloody-annoying reasonableness. God, he was such a sucker for letting himself get talked into these things. Par for the course, he told himself, for being such a chuffing team player. Yeah, the team benefitted - but what about him? It seemed as if his own personal needs or ambitions continually got put to the back of the queue.

Freddie'd been working here over twenty years, seen one marriage fail and another on the verge of failing. Been denied promotion to Brewery Manager when there had been a management buy-out a few years ago and the new ownership team - Arthur included - had divvied up the management roles nicely between them. He had more experience than any of them - and what did he have to show for it? Ever-bloody-reliable, doormat Freddie - everyone's dogsbody, willing to pitch in whenever and wherever needed to make sure the customers got their orders and the business made its numbers. Meanwhile, he was pulling down the same wage he'd been earning five years ago, had no promotion prospects in sight, and he wasn't getting any younger. That financial adviser bloke that Arthur had arrange to speak to all the staff after the last wave of pension fund changes had flipped through Freddie's figures and sucked his teeth. Sucked his chuffing teeth! Things carried on like this and Freddie'd have no teeth - and no retirement to enjoy them in neither.

"Driving the forklift!" he had exploded at Arthur's proposal. "Accidents are too chuffing easy as it is - that two-ton scuttleshit is an accident waiting to happen. And when it does, it won't just be miladdo who cops it - he could bring down the whole chuffing place, state it's in!"

Freddie was referring to the decaying and decrepit fabric of the brewery buildings that Arthur knew were rickety. The place was leased from the council and had been an abattoir before that. No-one had wanted to take it on when it was lying empty so the council had dropped the rent to peanuts and Arthur and his partners had jumped at the chance. But that had been years ago. And the place hadn't been in great shape even back then. Since the council received next to no money for the place, they weren't in a hurry to do it up; and since Arthur and his partners didn't own the building (and the council wouldn't sell it) they were unwilling to spend money on it without any return (plus the terms of the lease forbade them from doing so without council permission). So they were stuck in a negotiating stalemate which had been dragging on for years now. Meanwhile, the fabric of the buildings continued to deteriorate and the working conditions were gradually becoming more and more pathetic. One good storm would likely finish the place off. Arthur had smiled apologetically and raised his hands.

"Which is why I want you to train him, Freddie."

"Look, Arthur. If you want to give the little prick something to do, there's plenty of manual labour or simple stuff he could be doing. God knows. But the forklift? You need someone responsible doing that."

"He is responsible."

"Right. Whenever anything goes missing, he's responsible."

Arthur had bristled, gritted his teeth and then forced himself to stay calm. "Freddie. Sit down. Please." Freddie had been pacing the office, his agitation and unease clear from both his body language and his voice. He now reluctantly fell into a chair and Arthur leant back in his own and pressed his fingers together beneath his chin.

"Are you making a direct accusation, Freddie?"

"No." Freddie had almost curled up into a ball on the chair in front of him, a small child being asked a direct question by an adult.

"You are referring, no doubt, to the rumours circulating that the spate of petty thefts is all down to Tyler?"

"Yes."

"Do you have any evidence? Any? Of any kind, that could be used to corroborate your, or anyone else's, suspicions?"

Freddie paused for a moment. "No."

"Ok, then. So, let us persist with the old tradition of presuming innocence until guilt is proven, shall we? We will give Tyler - and all the other employees, yourself included - the benefit of the doubt until such time as irrefutable evidence emerges."

"Are you accusing me-"

"No, Freddie." Arthur raised his eyebrows, alarmed,

and rowed back. "I am not. Figure of speech. Just... for me, hmm? Show him the ropes? You're right we don't want accidents, which is why it's important - I think - to have an experienced operator like yourself train him up. How often are we short-handed here?"

"All the chuffing time." Freddie smiled, despite himself, shaking his head sadly.

"You know it. So, having an extra pair of hands - on tap - to pitch in. Valuable, huh?"

"Yeah." Freddie accepted. "It would be."

"And, if his hands are being kept busy working, they can't be busy elsewhere now, can they?"

"So you *do* think he-"

"No. I'm not saying that. But the devil finds work for idle hands, and all that. Let's not give him the opportunity, shall we?"

Freddie took a long, deep breath and exhaled slowly. "Ok. Where is the little arsehole?"

"Last time I saw him, he was having a fag leaning against the spent grain trailer." Arthur slid his fingers between the venetian blinds to squint out of the grimy window. "I can see a pair of feet there now. Guess it's him."

"Figures."

"Freddie? Go easy on him? He's just a kid."

"Kid my arse." And he shook his head sadly as he closed Arthur's office door.

Standing by the small packing desk at the far end of the warehouse, Freddie leant on it, pushing his full force through his arms into the desk and down onto the concrete floor. He looked at the flat-packed gift boxes leaning against the wall. Twelve bottles to a pack, the printed logo on the side: *The Biggar Little Brewery. Smaller batches for a Biggar taste.*

Jesus. So, Little Miss Perfect gets her runt trained up does she? And of course knight-in-shining-armour, ever-amorous, thinking-with-his-dick Arthur "Jurassic" Parke didn't want her to be disappointed in any way did he? Oh no. It was alright for the rest of the staff to be on chuffing piecework or zero-hour contracts but not her. Heaven forbid she got a ladder in her tights or snagged a chuffing nail. No, she had to be kept pampered and pristine until she got down on her knees and sucked Jurassic's dick dry.

And now he had the job of baby-sitting her insolent toerag son into the bargain.

"Oy, soft ollies!" Freddie barked over at the silhouetted figure of Tyler, skulking beyond the warehouse double-doors. "Get your arse in 'ere. There's work to be done."

Tyler shuffled over, his brewery baseball cap on backwards. Christ, look at him, he was walking with a pimp roll, like some kind of gangsta rapper who thought he was so chuffing cool.

"Right. Knocking off time just went back two hours, young 'un. Time to put your back into it."

"I do put my back into it." Tyler's resentment was palpable.

"I'm talking about your work ethic, not your sex life." Freddie sniped. "If you have one. Shaving yet?"

"Yes, thanks." Tyler sneered. "Do it every day. Shaving too."

"Yeah? Well, wanks don't count, sunshine. So get your hands off your cock and start paying attention. Boss says I'm to show you the ropes on the forklift and I'm a busy man, so I'm not going to repeat myself. With me?"

"Aye." Tyler responded, sullenly.

"Good. C'mon, then. Haven't got all day."

Arthur stood by the portable heater in his office and leant against the window, craning to see Freddie and Tyler by the forklift in the far corner. The warehouse was a draughty outbuilding separated from the main fermenting room by a large waterfall of heavy translucent plastic strips. On one side of this doorway were pallets loaded with six or eight kegs each, stacked in piles five layers high. The kegs were all coloured to indicate their contents, with one stack of pallets bearing a series of multi-coloured kegs, looking like the Jamaican flag. These were the special anniversary concoction - initially a brainchild of the head brewer, Damian, who was given licences to experiment and pursue his own ideas to both keep him sweet and, Arthur hoped, provide opportunity for serendipity to come calling and deliver a new, original flavour sensation that the marketing team could then go mad with to drum up a novelty name and label combination.

The last one had been *Hop To It* - a blend of chocolate malts that gave a darker, but sweeter taste, which they had marketed as an Easter special and given a cartoon bunny label with outsize ears. The current one was their *Hoppy Anniversary* special which they were pushing hard to create a closer tie with as many local pubs and hotels as they could before the big brewery chain from Glasgow and the West - rumoured to be eyeing Lanarkshire and the Borders for their next expansion - muscled in and stole the business from under their noses.

Freddie was now gesticulating with that permanently-aggrieved expression he assumed whenever he clocked on, and Tyler was standing with his hands in his pockets looking up, down and around - anywhere but where

Freddie was needing him to look. How could such a beautiful, bubbly, fantastic woman like Angela have a surly, sullen string-of-resentment son like Tyler? Arthur couldn't understand it.

He'd had always had his eye on Tyler, for different reasons at different ages.

To begin with he had almost been jealous of the baby and the adoration, and proximity to Angela's breasts, that the child could claim. The maternal softness and richness that enveloped Angela for that first year or so had driven Arthur to levels of wet dream which had led to bouts of self-medicated masturbation which, in turn, had left him with an unappealing skin outbreak on his penis. He had told his doctor that the soreness was an accidental exposure to some new enzyme liquid they were experimenting with at the brewery. His Doctor had simply said, "Of course it is" and given him a prescription for penicillin.

When the baby had become a toddler, Arthur had felt the need to keep an eye out all over the brewery. It was like being a new father, constantly assessing his living room for sharp edges or things which could be put into your mouth, but with the added problem of it being a work environment, with other people around, and limited control of room temperatures, dangerous substances, traffic and noise levels. Looking back he felt like he had been living on eggshells for a year while Tyler had got the measure of this environment and Arthur had stuck notices up all over the brewery reminding staff to take extra care because there was a small child around and to look out in case he escaped. It had been like working at Jurassic Park, worrying whether this precious creature would escape the confines of his carefully controlled paddock, the only difference being that rather than injure the other occupants this creature would harm himself. He had made reference to this to other staff, jokingly at the time, only to subsequently discover that this had become a nickname they used for him, behind his back.

Arthur had been so relieved once Tyler had started school, he felt that he had suffered disproportionate hair loss due to stress. But he returned during holidays, and even at an early age, Tyler had seemed to possess some kind of talent for schizophrenia. He could play happily and entertain himself. But if you took something from him, or denied him a request, it was like shadow passing over the sun. His face would darken in an instant, and then in a blink of an eye it would be gone. Arthur was never quite sure if it had ever been there but he saw it again and again - enough to be completely unnerved by it. But never enough to mention it to Angela who, it seemed to Arthur, had never seen it.

But over the years, it appeared that other staff witnessed this facial transformation too. Whispered conversations bearing Tyler's name would suddenly stop when Arthur walked into a room. Normally cheery staff would give Arthur anxious sideways glances in the tea room and, when he asked them if they were alright or wished them a cheery Good Afternoon, they would smile nervously and scurry back to their duties.

And, this past year, petty pilfering had become a thing. It had started with Patti on reception claiming that she had lost a pair of earrings, then Mike began checking the levels of petty cash and was convinced there were weekly discrepancies, and there was a steady disappearance of bottles and crates from the onsite shop. Arthur had posted notices around the place saying, PLEASE DON'T

LEAVE YOUR PERSONAL POSSESSIONS IN PLAIN SIGHT and someone had scrawled underneath one of them: CLEVER GIRL. Underneath another: CRIME, UH, FINDS A WAY. When a weekly stock take seemed to show that over 50 bottles had vanished and Freddie was convinced that two kegs had gone walkies from the warehouse over the Christmas period, Arthur had no choice but to step in.

He didn't mention this, or any of his concerns, to Angela. He had just arranged for some CCTV cameras to be installed and now he had asked Freddie to give Tyler something to engage him. Oh, but his mother, Angela. What a sensuous, gentle, loving soul she was! Eyes like liquid chocolate, hair like waving barley, a voice like heather honey, an intoxicating smile, an aroma of soft femininity. One glance from Angela could warm your heart and melt your brain. Angela was a heady brew indeed.

"Arthur?"

Arthur clutched at his heart involuntarily as he was jolted from his daydreaming and momentarily couldn't work out where he was or what had happened. He felt his face cold against the glass and pulled back from the window, turning towards the door.

Patti was standing there with her eyebrows raised. Arthur wasn't sure which of them was the more surprised or startled. "CCTV man's here."

"Right, you are." Arthur cleared his throat, and checked that the front of his trousers was decent enough for him to emerge from behind his chair.

"Where do you want all this, then?" The workman

brought his trolley piled with boxes to a stop, wiped his nose on a sleeve of his once-white overalls and sniffed loudly.

"Well, I was rather hoping you could tell me." Arthur smiled hopefully, waving his arm somewhat vaguely around the draughty warehouse area.

"Not my department, guv. Do as I'm told, that's me. You want er... advice. That's extra. Consultancy is that. Head Office."

"Consultancy?"

"Yep. Not my department."

"Yes. So you said." Arthur wrinkled up his nose and scratched his neck behind one ear. "Well, you see it all rather depends on the scope really."

"Scope?"

"Yes, well there are certain... hotspots I suppose. Places which I would like to be monitored."

"'Nuf said. Point me at 'em."

"Yes, but I need to know that having a camera mounted in a specific position will monitor the scene I need, well, monitoring."

"Ah, gotcha." The man wiped and sniffed again. "Well, you show me where you want monitoring and I'll tell you where I can mount 'em. See, it's not just a case of coverage - that's what we call it, in the trade. Coverage - it's also about where we can run power to 'em an' that."

"I see."

"Then there's the issue of where you position your server. 'Cos you'll need it connecting to your network."

"Network?" The tiny start of a bad feeling was germinating in Arthur's gut.

"Yeah. You want to be able to see the images on computer screens don'cha?"

"Well, yes."

"Well the cameras are connected to a server and the server needs to be connected to your network so that the other computers on your network can talk to the server and see the pictures."

Arthur was now moving sweatily outside his comfort zone. "But we don't have a network."

"Eh?" The workman frowned and pulled a pair of crumpled xerox'd sheets from the back pocket of his overalls. "Says here you got wifi."

"Oh yes, we have wifi." Arthur said, relieved.

"Well that's a network then, innit?" The workman smiled. "Mind you, also says here you've been quoted for a wired connection, not a wireless one."

"Is that a problem?"

"No. Not a problem. It's extra, though, if you want wireless."

"Do I want wireless?"

"Well, that depends where you put your server!" The man grinned broadly, in what Arthur considered a quite unnecessary display of good humour. Like someone who rolls down their window when you're trying to find a parking space and shouts happily "They're all taken!"

"Right. Well, perhaps we can come back to that? So, for instance, I'd like a camera to be able to cover this area here."

The workman cast his eyes around the space, with its scruffy whitewashed walls, the corrugated roof inlaid with ancient cobwebbed skylights. "You got your tall ceiling here. Rafters an' that. We can run the cables along them and down to a power socket somewhere. Is there a power socket somewhere?" He looked wildly round, rather optimistically Arthur thought.

"It's a brewery warehouse. An old brewery warehouse. Used to be an abattoir, actually. Place is a bit decrepit, if I'm being-"

"Yeah, but you got another office over there aint'cha?" The workman interrupted. "Got power in there do ya?"

"Well, the light's on."

"Means you got power. Doesn't mean you got a power socket." The workman smiled. "I can fit you a new one if you don't."

"Is that extra also?"

"Yep."

"Thought so." Arthur sighed.

"Arthur!" Patti's head appeared cheerily through the open door to the admin corridor. She raised her eyebrows, her voice a bright stage whisper. "The Police are here."

"What? Oh. Er." Arthur was flummoxed. He looked at the stupidly smiling workman waiting for further instruction. "Look, I'm afraid I'm quite busy at the moment. Perhaps if you could have a word with my Foreman over there?" He nodded over to the small packing station where Freddie was standing, flipping through a printout. "He could show you the best places for... coverage... and you could start putting the cameras up and do all the necessary... connection stuff. And then come and get me if there's a problem?"

The workman sniffed, unimpressed. "What about extras?"

"Yes, well. If any are needed, I'm sure Freddie can deal with that. Freddie!" Arthur shouted across the echoing space and Freddie looked over. "CCTV man's here!" And Arthur scurried away back to his office to see what the Police might want.

Freddie couldn't chuffing believe it. He only had one pair of eyes and he was using both of them right now: keeping one on miladdo currently trying to guide the forklift between two piles of empty pallets like he was being asked to check someone's prostate; and the other on the stock-take sheets which, again, were showing discrepancies. Now Arthur had wafted some chuffer towards him and scurried off, leaving muggins here to deal with this upselling arsehole wearing overalls and a chuffing perma-grin.

Their initial conversation had been brief and now the CCTV man sniffed, offended. "Top of the line stuff this, you know. We only stock the best."

"Yes, well I can tell it's chuffing top-of-the-line from the chuffing top-of-the-line price, can't I?" Freddie wasn't going to let the man's patter get through his own natural chumminess-shield. "Don't you have anything a little less thousand-y?"

"Well, you see, the problem is that this quote here." The man waved the two xeroxed sheets airily. "Been done by some eejit up at Head Office, clearly doesn't know what they're doing. I can see with my own two eyes that it's all wrong for what you need. You have been misled is all."

"That's as chuffing maybe, pal. But my boss - the arse who pushed you over here, him? He has approved this quote and, between you and me, getting *any* money spent on this place is a minor chuffing miracle. We're only a small outfit you know. Not made of money. So, what I'm looking for is something which will work for us that'll fit into this chuffing quote."

"No extras?" The man's face fell.

"No extras." Freddie folded his arms and waited.

"Right." The man sucked his teeth. "Give me a minute."

Arthur Parke was a good man, a kind man. A gentle man and a gentleman. Thoughtful, sensitive, honest, caring, cheery, who looked for the good in everyone and was optimistic about the future and the prospects for the human race.

In other words, a complete sucker.

From childhood to his current late middle-age, when he really should have known better and at least learnt from experience, he had fallen prey to the petty, the dishonest and the criminal. All who could take advantage of him seemed to do so, as if his openness and hope shone like some kind of beacon above his head, flashing the word "Victim" in all directions. And, like trick-or-treaters attracted by a doorstep filled with beautifully carved pumpkins, the chancers and the scammers came calling. They recognised a quality victim when they saw one. And Arthur was quality all the way down.

He was a middle-sized, middle-aged man, not too tall, not too short. Unremarkable features, where nothing was outrageous or distinctive, arranged in such a way to make him always look a little sunken and lop-sided - as if someone had taken a souffle out of the oven a fraction too early. He had a fleshy nose, slightly askew, bright blue eyes which could twinkle in delight or sink into empathetic sadness beneath his beetle brows, and thick lips which concealed a generous array of somewhat crooked teeth. His complexion was ever-so-slightly pockmarked, such that you were never quite sure if it wasn't just some trick of the light, and his soft voice had a tiny wobble to it which only served to lend him more sincerity and kindliness than he had any use for.

Arthur was losing his hair and gaining a waistline like many a businessman who took insufficient exercise, insufficient care of their health, partook of too many business lunches or drained minibars on expenses. He had always meant to watch his weight, take care of himself, and as the years had advanced, hoped against hope that he would attract a wife before his weight got out of hand. But the hope and the motivation were no match for his lack of willpower. Weekly, he would draw up a shopping list of fruit, pulses and herbal tea and head steadfastly to the supermarket, intent on sticking to a meal plan and a healthy diet, only to find himself stuffing Scotch Eggs and Haagen-Dazs into his bag at the checkout. He didn't know he had done it, somewhere between parking the car and entering the store, a blanket fell across his mind and he sleep-walked around the aisles and only woke up again when he had swiped his card.

Thus was a typical big shop for Arthur, and thus was his life.

He was a sucker for weepies and nostalgia, musicals and happy endings, sad songs and rom-coms. No Big Issue went unsold, no tin-shaker unpassed, no Oxfam bag unstuffed. The Little Biggar Brewery contributed regularly to the local football team, rugby team, weekly open-air market, annual town festival, fireworks and High Street Christmas lights. They donated crates of beer to raffles, tombolas, Rainbows, Brownie and Scout troops, harvest festivals and school fetes. Arthur's partners in the business had given up complaining about the effect on their bottom line and accepted that there was at least some value in the immense social capital and goodwill the brewery built up as a result of all this philanthropy.

As a result, Arthur represented all that was good and noble about the business and could be relied upon to be the happy, smiling, munificent face of grasping capitalism while behind him his fellow managers could smile thinly about corporate social responsibility while they counted the cold hard cash. Whenever there were layoffs, or slowdowns or any bad news to be borne, his partners would wheel Arthur out to do his stuff and explain in pained, genuine, caring tones why this was regrettably necessary and that it was an ugly but unavoidable fact.

Everyone loved Arthur - just no-one loved him enough to want to share their life with him. And he knew it.

God knows he'd looked hard enough.

Once it became abundantly clear that there were no willing and eligible matrons in the local area, he had scolded himself for being so unambitious and gone online in search of love. What he had found had delighted him: an unexpected procession of beautiful women, mostly considerably younger than himself and all impossibly glamorous. The female populace of the Biggar-Broughton-Skirling triangle couldn't hope to compete with the bounty available from his own computer keyboard.

Each lady in turn would express their undying affection for him and desire to meet him, love him and spend the rest of their life with him. If only they weren't so very far away. Or labouring under the supreme difficulty of obtaining a visa. Or unable to escape from their current undercover assignment without having to buy themselves out in some way.

Even sending them money to assist them out of their difficulties hadn't helped and Arthur had found that, one after another, either further insurmountable problems had resulted and they had sadly had to give up their dream of coming to the UK, or regrettably take their leave due to family bereavements. In one tragic case (he later found out from another woman) one of his earlier girlfriends, Mathilde, hadn't disappeared but had been murdered by a jealous ex-boyfriend.

Whatever the detail, the pattern was always the same - not a single one of these relationships had lasted or even transformed into a physical one. Each had started out as a promising opportunity, blossomed into a rich potential which had him floating daily on air, only for life to cruelly puncture his inflatable and leave him watching distraught from the shoreline as his potential partner sank out of sight, waving a tearful farewell.

Oh, all those poor, poor women. Although, many of them hadn't been poor at all. Not financially anyway. They had all been quite wealthy, just temporarily unable to access their money due to circumstances beyond their control. He hoped, with the exception of Mathilde, they were all now at least safe and healthy and had finally managed to gain possession of the riches that events had previously denied them.

Which reminded him: he hadn't heard back from that Nigerian Prince recently.

"Ok. This is just the job for you." The CCTV man had returned from his van with a brightly coloured box, still in shrink, and plonked it on the packing station.

"Yeah?" Freddie waited, not optimistically, to be impressed.

"The XC-1100." The man's smile had returned and he

started stripping away the shrink-wrap to open the box. "New on the market."

"How much?" Freddie wanted to nip this in the bud.

"Don't worry about the price right now. We can do this on appro."

"Appro?"

"Yeah. Look." The man lowered his voice and cast his eyes around the empty warehouse as if about to divulge a state secret. "You're trying to catch someone at it, right? But you don't know what they're going to half-inch next. And you can't afford to put cameras up left right and centre 'cos you're a small outfit. Correct?"

"Correct." Freddie nodded in agreement, despite himself.

"So, this little cutie, you can stick it anywhere see. Rechargeable battery, wifi connectivity, motion activated. Put it in one place, leave it. If nothing happens it'll just sit there. Won't come on. Move it somewhere else, wait and see. If it detects motion in its coverage field it'll automatically start recording. Battery'll give you a week of recording. Almost."

"A week! How much chuffing tape is that?"

"Doesn't use tape!" The man grinned. "This the twenty-first century mate. Straight to disk. On the server. All you need to do is check the camera schedule - you'll see if any video was recorded. Then you can just play it back on the monitor."

"What monitor?"

"The monitor on the server!" The man shook his head. "And if it hasn't done the job for you in, ooh, four weeks, you can give it back. No charge!"

"And if it has?"

The workman passed him a slip of paper and Freddie

pulled a face. "Chuffing hell. Any way we can knock the price down of summat else? Take the edge off this if we end up having to pay?"

"Well..." The man thoughtfully waggled his head from side to side. "We could save a fair bit if you put the server where there's already power and network connectivity. Shorter runs from the other cameras would help too."

"Such as?"

"Well, there." The man pointed to the small hutch of a room with the tiny lit window to one side of the warehouse door.

"I use that as my office."

"And?"

"Fine." Freddie sighed, resignedly.

From outside the open sliding warehouse doors there suddenly came the sound of a collision and many pallets crashing to the ground.

"Chuff's sake. Stick it in there. For now. I'll come and look at it when you're done." He wheeled and charged out of the warehouse, already yelling at the still invisible Tyler.

"Just in here, officers."

Arthur breezed in to the small cabin which Freddie called his office, followed by two policemen in uniform, their caps in their hands. Along with Freddie's desk newly-crammed with a large computer screen, a big beige box humming beneath it and the still partially unwrapped XC-1100 in front of him, the office was now officially overcrowded.

"S'alright Arthur. No need to knock." Freddie sniped.

"Sorry, Freddie." Arthur smiled apologetically and then noticed the new equipment on Freddie's desk. "Wasn't this stuff supposed to go in my office?"

Freddie returned the smile. "Extras."

"Ah, right. Ok." Arthur nodded. "Well, officers, this is it. Newly installed today as you can see."

The lead officer leant over and scanned the screen layout in front of Freddie, running his eyes across what he saw quite expertly. Freddie watched him and his partner, curiously: two young policemen looking like they had only just acquired their newly-minted uniforms. The other officer still stood on the threshold, gazing idly over his shoulder at something of interest in the warehouse.

"What's this all about?" Freddie resented the intrusion. It wasn't officially his office - wasn't officially anything other than a storeroom which he had acquired by stealth over the years, until it had become his *defacto* office. If he couldn't have the post of Brewery Manager, Freddie figured, at least he could acquire some of the trappings.

"Standard visit, Mr...?"

"Hughes."

The officer in the doorway suddenly woke up and scribbled in his notebook.

"I asked for security advice, Freddie. After the last time." Arthur said to Freddie, as if in cahoots.

"Always happy to assist when the public want advice on security." The lead officer smiled. "Perhaps, Mr Hughes, Mr Parke. Whilst you're both here, you could just help us with something else we're pursuing?"

"Oh aye?" Freddie looked up at Arthur who shrugged and raised his eyebrows.

"Yes. We're investigating a series of thefts at pubs in the surrounding area. All customers of yours, as it happens." The policeman flipped open his notebook. "The thefts - perhaps I should say, attempted thefts - all took place at the time of a delivery from this brewery."

Arthur's eyes widened and before he could stop himself he had blurted out "I hope you're not suggesting Angela could have anything to do with-?"

"Who's Angela?"

"Angela McKenna. Our delivery driver."

"I'm sure it's just a coincidence." He made a note in his book. "But we would like to speak to her - as a potential witness. If you could let us have her home address?"

Arthur nodded. "Yes. Of course."

Freddie stifled a laugh. "Wouldn't be too sure about it being a chuffing coincidence myself."

"Freddie!" Arthur bristled.

"Why do you say that, Mr Hughes?" The officer was immediately alert.

"Her chuffing son, Tyler. Sent him home early not long ago. Useless chuffing-"

"Freddie." Arthur attempted a gentle scolding. "Just because he doesn't know the ropes yet, doesn't mean-"

"Arthur, you may think the sun shines out of her arse, but I wouldn't let that little shite out of my sight, personally." Arthur's eyes bulged and he glared at Freddie, but Freddie ignored him. "And there's plenty others here who'd say the same."

"Is that right?"

"Aye, chuffing right. He'd be the first name in my notebook if I was you." Freddie stuck his chin out by way of emphasis. Arthur gritted his teeth and silently shook his head in denial.

"Mr Hughes. You wouldn't happen to know if Tyler McKenna owns a motorcycle, by any chance would you?"

"Wouldn't chuffing think so!" Snorted Freddie.

"May I ask why you're so sure?"

Freddie laughed. "Little toerag couldn't steer his dick into his trousers, never mind a motorbike. Not if the way he handles that chuffing forklift is anything to go by."

FOUR

Cullen stopped halfway up the climb over the pass in the hills to Stobo, sat on a pile of felled timber just off the trail, and looked back over the valley. The brewery lay peacefully in the soft evening light, the last of the day's warmth slowly rising towards the sky. But Cullen wasn't seeing it.

He was seeing a pair of dead, implacable eyes. Eyes that looked clean through you, like you were an invisible piece of shit, not worth wasting photons on. The kid had looked like he'd seen it all and couldn't give a fuck anymore. Cullen didn't believe in reincarnation. The idea bothered him. *He* didn't want to come back - not to this life. But he didn't think anyone could have eyes like that and not have lived a long vicious life of evil.

But, though this bothered him, something else disturbed him much, much more. Something less reachable, sitting out there just beyond the grasp of his recall. Cullen closed his eyes and reached for it.

He had seen eyes like that once before.

A young man had come to the door, back when Cullen had still been on the Force. A small, dingy council flat, several floors up in a dismal block. Graffiti and the smell of urine decorating the stairwells and the landings. He had opened the door, wearing a vest and jeans and an evil smile beneath that black mirror stare. Cullen had caught a glimpse of a heavily pregnant girl, even younger than the man, lurking in the background over his shoulder, calling out to ask who was at the door. But his eyes were dragged back to this man's face, a sullen dead-eyed look of casual, dismissive malevolence - a conviction that nothing could touch him and nothing mattered.

Cullen had later shown him how wrong he was.

Angela was always tired, often exhausted. When she managed to find a moment to sit quietly and think, it would only take one little thing to send her off down some dark, depressing rabbit-hole where she questioned everything and came up with no answers other than that she felt a failure. Working two jobs and caring for Tyler - and even now he was on the edge of manhood, make no mistake, he still needed caring for. Cleaning, cooking, laundry. She would work tirelessly to provide and maintain, looking for some sign from him that he appreciated it, or even noticed it. The most she got was the occasional tight smile or merest nod of the head. It was as if her son had decided that communicating with the world outside his head was a waste of energy - energy he could better husband and expend on worthwhile things like… well, she had to admit to herself during these moments of sad reflection, that she didn't really seem to know her son at all.

It hadn't always been like that, so her first inclination was always that she had somehow screwed up. The one job she had in life, her role as a mother, was what defined her. What she lived and breathed for. And yet the sole product of all that love and effort and care and hope was an unresponsive, some would say sullen, teenager who showed his mother as little affection or attention as possible. She tried to remember when he was smaller, more active, curious. Had he been a lively little boy, hungry for knowledge and fun and love, and somehow she had missed it?

She couldn't seem to conjure up images of Tyler as a child, now. Instead this same daydream sequence kept returning to her, blocking out everything else. She was on a windy, empty platform waiting on a train. A small child (perhaps Tyler, perhaps not) clutching her hand tightly, saying "Mummy, Mummy! Look, look!" He wanted her attention, her praise, her love. But she was focussing all her attention on the horizon, searching for that train. "Not now" She says. "Once we get on the train."

And every time she looks down, the child is a little older, a little more withdrawn. And she stands on that platform, wondering. Worrying but not doing anything. Thinking: What if, by the time the train comes, the child is a teenager and doesn't want to show me love anymore? What if, next time I look down, the child has grown up and left? What if, maybe... just maybe, that train never turns up at all? What if, I end my days on that platform all alone, wishing I'd spent more time in the here and now with the child at my side, instead of looking down that track for the train that never came?

And then the oven timer would sound and Angela would sleepwalk into the kitchen and take the pie out.

Tyler's father, Iain, had been a wrong'un, and Angela had known it from the first. She just couldn't help herself. Maybe it had been teenage rebellion, maybe it had been hormones and his chiselled features and his insouciant manner, maybe it had just been an attempt to kick back at her smothering parents and say "fuck it." Which she did, and thus Tyler was conceived.

Her relationship with Iain was never smooth - if it was smooth she was after she would have chased after Michael Ainsworth instead. He was Headboy, smart, suave and everything a girl's mother would have wanted in her daughter's boyfriend. But Michael was too neat, too nice, too... vacant. There was more in an Easter Egg. He had no rough edges, no cool remarks. Kissing him, she imagined, would have been like being nuzzled by Tim Brooke-Taylor's spaniel. She wanted danger and adventure and drama and risk - she wanted to feel alive - and Iain ticked all those boxes

He was a teenage dream: experienced, knowledgeable, tough. He could protect her - he had been the cool, hard kid at school that bullies stayed away from and who wouldn't go looking for trouble, but could handle himself if it found him. And he could pay for her - he was an apprentice plasterer and was bringing in a decent wage, cash in hand, every week. Iain was almost twenty, accessible adulthood made flesh. He was all hers and she fell for him. Hard.

But not as hard as he would hit her.

Oh, he had apologised and bought her chocolates, sworn he'd never do it again and said he knew it was his fault. And Angela forgave him and told herself it was a solitary moment of madness, he'd been drunk, tired, unaware of what he was doing. Until he did it again. This time he had meant business. Not some off-hand slap which had stung mentally and physically - this had been a beating. In anger. They had rowed about the coming baby and the costs that were starting to mount up - eating into Iain's weekly wage. He made a tidy sum but he had never been a saver and Angela was still at school. Once her parents had thrown her out and disowned her, they were suddenly on their own. A flat was needed, food, bills, all that was enough. But then infant paraphernalia, more furniture, sterilising stuff and bottles and nappies and wipes and on and on and on. Iain took to going to the pub to avoid coming home to more requests for stuff. And the more he drank, the more resentful he became and the more easily he found a way to justify his bitterness so that it easily twisted and festered into anger at the slightest provocation. And Angela found it so, so easy to unconsciously provoke him: asking him about his day, cooking him dinner, snuggling in on the sofa. It was all too much for him. Too smothering. He was choking and needed air.

And then one day a police detective came to the door looking for him, and away he went. Angela never saw or heard from Iain again. She had no idea what happened to him. She contacted the police but they claimed not to know anything about him. She asked his friends, checked with his work, his parents. He had disappeared off the map and no-one knew when, or if, he was coming back.

So, eight months pregnant and just about to turn eighteen, Angela was alone, expelled from school, parentless, homeless and about to become a single mum.

She built a life for herself and her son. Slowly, painstakingly and tenaciously. Working whenever she could, night and day, falling back on the kindness of friends and neighbours to look after Tyler, living on the knock-off supermarket shelves and charity shops, carboot and rummage sales. She had housing benefit, maternity benefit, child benefit and income support. She managed. It was grim and it was tough and she felt that she was ageing at an astonishing rate. The idea, and memory, of getting dressed up and having a night out some vague, foggy dream of someone else's life - certainly no longer hers.

By the time she was twenty she was at least keeping her head above water, even if it was falling into the sink every time she got home. Tyler's cries and cuddles were sustenance enough and she survived on that. Just.

Mostly because she had an unlikely guardian angel, in the shape of Arthur Parke. She had started working at the Brewery as an admin/receptionist/dogsbody and, as the business had been slowly but discernibly declining, she had increasingly taken on other's tasks when staff left the company, all in search of a little extra money or a little more overtime. Nothing strenuous, but she had stood in for the delivery driver, Eric, when he had been unwell, and Renee who did payroll, after she had retired.

With the management buyout there had been an influx of new owners, a more professional approach to running a business, and a changing of the management guard. One of the new bosses' wives was trained in Accounts, another was a marketing and branding expert who wasn't afraid to man the sparsely visited reception desk and answer the phones. That left Angela without portfolio, until Arthur had suggested she take on the mantle as the sole, permanent delivery driver. She had protested due to the fact that it wasn't guaranteed five-days-a-week and it also meant she couldn't have Tyler by her side. She couldn't afford childcare and working in the nice warm office had allowed her to have a wee playpen and cot for him where she could keep an eye on him and know he was safe.

Never mind, Arthur had said. You can have him in your cab and they had rigged up a child's carseat and installed a special harness to ensure it met all necessary safety regulations. But what about five-days-a-week? Ah, Arthur had said, Yes we can't guarantee that, but we are moving ahead with ambitious plans to develop new product lines, new customers and targetting larger upscale clients who will give us a more predictable and healthy pipeline of orders. Angela had been dubious and concerned, but Arthur was one of the few, kindly honest men you could trust. He didn't have a mean bone in his body. How anyone could ever mistrust him or fail to confide in him, she simply never knew.

But there was much Angela never knew.

She never knew how much Arthur had had to fight and negotiate and argue for those little kindnesses and gestures and commitments for her which had made it possible for her to stay. She would never know how much Arthur watched her from his office window as she carried Tyler on her hip to the cab and hoisted him up into his car seat, her short jacket riding up and exposing her smooth, snapped-back-into-shape midriff. The way she tucked a persistently stray strand of hair behind one ear when she was trying to fasten the seatbelt, the way she licked her top lip with the tip of her tongue when she was checking the delivery manifest, the way she pulled funny faces in the rear-view mirror when she was putting on lipstick before setting off.

She never knew how close she had become to being laid off when the new orders didn't materialise, or how much of her "overtime" pay went unrecorded on the payroll records because it came out of Arthur's own pocket.

But one thing she did know. She had grown to love, love, love her job as delivery driver. As she bounced down country roads, her son burbling happily in the seat beside her, the sun shining and a whole day of driving through bonny Borders' scenery, she would think of Iain, sometimes with gratitude, sometimes with remorse, but mostly with a bitter-sweet combination of joy and sadness when she looked at her son's face. He had his father's eyes and mouth, her nose and chin, and there was something in the liveliness of his gaze when he looked up at her in the cab that made her heart shoot through her ribcage. Those huge, round, inky eyes which seemed liquid and rich and fiercely intelligent. Even before Tyler could speak she knew he was going to be smart. A winner. A son to be proud of.

And he would be her son. Only hers. Iain had forfeited the right to be associated with Tyler the moment he had buggered off. She would sometimes have nightmares, when she could manage to sleep at all, where he reappeared one day on her doorstep and Tyler would fly down the hall, arms outstretched, crying "Daddy! Daddy!" and Iain would scoop him up into his arms, swirl him round high in the air and then the pair would stride off while Angela stood, chained to the spot, unable to call out or make a sound, and struggling to do anything while her son and his father disappeared down the end of the street and turned the corner for ever.

She would wake, crying, her nose streaming, her breath ragged in great heaving gulps. It always felt so real and it would take a few days of telling herself that this was just a nightmare: Iain had gone, years ago. Tyler was hers, and she was his. And that was all there was to it.

And she told herself this every day, as she looked at her son, her chest bursting with love and pride. She didn't need to worry. Her son would never leave her, never not love her. Never hurt her the way Iain had.

Never.

"What were you doing humping barrels in the first place?" Cullen asked.

"Davy's short-handed. I'm a regular. On a Tuesday." Paul waved an arm loftily around the pub as if he had part-ownership.

Paul, also known as Big Paul, sometimes abbreviated to BP and then further to Beep, was not a small man. Broad, stocky, massive, huge. These were adjectives which meant little when you stood them up next to the man and saw how they paled against his frame and heft. He was 6'5", a little more with the wind behind him, and whilst his weight had varied wildly in the past - once even ballooning past the twenty-one stone mark - with the advent of his relationship with Shirley it had gradually settled into a healthier eighteen-nineteen stone bracket. Shirley called this health-management: keeping her man fitter and his lifestyle more compatible with her ambition of seeing out a ripe old age together; Paul called it mithering - albeit not to her face. His strategy for coping with imposed fried-food deprivation and processed-meat portion control was to smile lovingly and resolve to bolt a couple of pasties down at the next petrol station forecourt.

So this man-mountain's stature may have screamed "Beware!" but when you looked into his face and beheld the broad, beaming smile and big brown eyes which glistened in his smooth olive-skinned face, your senses translated this as "Big Ted" and you instantly relaxed into the company of a man whose hands were rough and hard from the carpenter's trade but whose heart was gentle, honest and kind.

And who often had a raging thirst on him.

Cullen pulled an incredulous face. "Only Tuesdays?"

"Alright, Wednesdays, Thursdays and Fridays an' all." Paul relented. "But Tuesday's delivery day."

Cullen smirked. "Busy Mondays then?"

"Smartarse." Paul sneered. "I'm a mate, as well as a good customer. One hand washes the other." Paul swigged down the last half of his drink and wiped his mouth extravagantly on his sleeve.

"With beer?" Cullen questioned, arching one eyebrow.

"Cash as well. He needs some odd jobs doing - maintenance, running repairs, whitewashing. Like that."

"Branching out from joinery then?"

"Not really. My battery's on its arse."

"Battery?"

"In the van. Fecker won't start. Need a new one." Paul gave a tight smile. "Bit short, right now."

"You don't say."

"Aye, well. Can't reliably get anywhere so wanted something handy, earn a few quid, replace my battery."

"And a few free pints." Cullen smiled in understanding.

"It's good stuff, this. Centenary brew. *Hoppy Anniversary* it says, look!" He swivelled the bottle round so that Cullen could see the label, as proud as if he'd brewed it himself. "Glad I helped Davy bring it in. It's on special you know."

"Hmm." Cullen could not have appeared less interested. Paul didn't let that trouble him. The last thing you did with Cullen was go by appearances. It wasn't what he said, or how he looked - it was what he didn't say and what he did that you had to watch out for. Reading between the lines might just get you to Point A, but typically by then Cullen was already at Point D, heading for Point G with a secret plan to get to Point P.

You would end up there too, in the end, and just as you were working out how it had all happened, Cullen would be off and gone and you wouldn't see him again until the next time. Whenever that would be. You had to go all-in, play your cards blind and trust that Cullen knew what was best. Fortunately, this was fine by Paul. He was not the demanding type. *Trust the soup* was Paul's attitude: everything will be alright in the end so, if it's not alright, it's not yet the end. His role was to be ever-reliable, ever-trustworthy, ever-ready. If you needed someone to step up to the plate, Paul was your man - as long as the plate had some bacon on it.

And Cullen was here now, looking for Paul. Which meant he had a plan. Which meant... well, Paul wasn't sure what it meant - other than it was an opportunity to get some free beer.

"Special as in specially-brewed and labelled. Just for Davy." Paul wished to impress upon his friend just how honoured he was to be drinking this particular concoction - partially to show Cullen how clued-in he was with the goings-on around him (not something Paul could usually brag about, or indeed even comment on) and also in the vain hope that Cullen might indulge him with another free drink.

He didn't.

"Oh aye." Cullen said, summoning all the interest of someone being asked to select their favourite dog shit.

"Aye. Well, not just for Davy you understand. That would be a bit much, wouldn't it? No, I mean it's the brewery's centenary. Or summat. You know, anniversary of the first time they... did summat. Whatever. Detail. Point is, they have created this one-off blend and only pubs that are long-standing customers in the local-"

"I'll stick to this."

Paul pulled a face. "What IS that?"

"Water."

"Man, you can do better than that."

"It's water, Beep. Water. Healthy, simple, pure."

"From Davy's tap?" Paul winced. "Plus, you do realise that 100% of people who drink water end up dead."

"Seriously?"

"Straight up. Water is the silent killer." Paul nodded, case closed. "Never touch it."

"Right. Just beer for you then?"

"Don't look at me like that. Beer's one of your five a day."

"Along with...?"

"Well, bacon. Obv." Paul tapped meaningfully on his glass and gave the matter some thought. "Erm..."

"Ok, I'll buy you another. If you explain how beer is one of your five a day."

"Easy! Beer is made from hops. And barley. Barley and hops are plants. QED." Paul beamed. "Beer is basically liquid salad."

Cullen sighed. "QED, huh?"

"Never mind that." Paul waggled his empty bottle in Cullen's direction. "Same again."

When Cullen returned with another drink, Paul gratefully swallowed most of it and then began regaling him with a significantly embellished version of the events from the other day.

Cullen interrupted. "A leftie you say?"

"Aye. Although I can't speak for his politics." Paul replayed the scene in his mind's eye now, to confirm that the biker had indeed held the knife aloft in their left hand.

Satisfied he had it correct, he nodded to himself and made to finish the rest of his beer.

"Did he have dead eyes?" Cullen interjected.

"What?"

"You know, dead eyes. Eyes that kind of looked through you and didn't give a shit."

"Who?"

"Your leftie with the knife."

"I don't know! He had a helmet on." Paul was irritated that he had now lost his train of thought.

"Anyone else see him?"

"No-one else round was there, first thing?"

"First thing meaning...?"

"Well, ten I guess."

"Can't you be precise? Be better than guesswork."

"It's precision guesswork!" Paul cast his mind back. "It was just gone ten. Pub wasn't even open!"

"Hmm."

"Why does it matter anyway?"

"Dead eyes. Left-handed. Motorbike helmet." Cullen intoned, ticking off some mental list.

"I just said, I didn't see his eyes!" Paul sighed, getting as close to exasperation as he could, which was usually a long way away. Paul was not the exasperated type, more the type to generate exasperation in others, and it was unusual for Cullen to be so... unusual. "What's with all this dead eye stuff?"

"Maybe nothing."

"Maybe nothing?"

"Aye."

Paul screwed his face up, but Cullen ignored him, his pupils zigzagging as he wandered alone in his thoughts.

"Build?"

"Uh. Skinny." Then, remembering his embellished story, Paul corrected himself. "I mean, athletic. Wiry. Plenty of speed and agility."

"Fast?"

"And strong. He was very strong. Surprisingly so."

"For one so slight?" Cullen's arched eyebrow could have been indicating scepticism or intrigue. Paul plumped for the latter.

"Aye. He leapt up, despite me throwing that keg at him, and shot away like nobody's business. Fit and athletic, I'd say." Paul considered. "Maybe he's a pro-wrestler?"

"Or young."

"Oh." Paul's face dropped. "Aye, may be more likely that."

When Tyler came home it was almost dark. Angela had tried distracting herself by making an over-elaborate meal, fussing and preparing in the kitchen, all bustle and purpose. Then she had sat trance-like in the living room, watching the light fade while the dinner slowly burnt in the oven.

"Where have you been?" She rose, her agitation zipping from a simmer to a rolling boil at his nonchalant entrance. Tyler could do that to people, she knew, like he was some kind of catalyst. She loved him, totally and completely, but she was under no illusions that her son had some innate ability to ignite fear or loathing in other people merely by his physical presence. She had often wondered whether it was pheremonal or something - an odour which was undetectable but that people unconsciously picked up and had them instantly on their guard.

"Work." Tyler droned. It was difficult to get an

enthusiastic or even multi-syllabic response from her son at the best of times, teenagers being what they were. Boys especially. Expecting a cheery wave and an engaging smile from a seventeen year-old male was like hoping to wake up next to an Infinity Stone.

"The police were here today."

"What?" Suddenly there was fire in her son's eyes, as if someone had just plugged him in. Angela gawped at the transformation and a sharp memory flashed through her head, leaving her momentarily breathless. In the space she left, Tyler prodded: "What did you tell them?"

"What do you mean? What is there to tell?"

"Nothing."

"Tyler?" Angela looked askew at her son. "What do you think they were here for?"

"Nothing."

This wasn't what she had expected. Their interest in Tyler had been confined to a few questions tagged on to the end of their conversation with her. Angela had assumed they were innocent, an afterthought, and that her son would be as bemused as she was by their interest in her and him. Apparently she was dead wrong. "Why? What's this all about?"

"Nothing."

"Nothing? The police come here and clearly there is some reason for it that you - and they - aren't telling me. What the hell is going on, Tyler?"

"Nothing, Mum." Her son was still animated and visibly alert. She was going to get to the bottom of this.

"Don't *nothing* me, Tyler McKenna. What have you done?"

"I haven't done anything!" He was actually gesticulating now and raising his voice, his jet black eyes flashing angrily. "Why do you assume I've done anything? Why is it always me?"

"What do you mean, always you? When have I ever accused you of anything? Always you. What are you on about? And I think, when you are wanted by the police, it is a fair assumption that you have done something. Something wrong!"

"I haven't done anything." He repeated, gritting his teeth, his face hard and menacing. Tyler turned and headed for the stairs.

"Don't you go anywhere without giving me an explanation, young man!" Angela was caught between being furious and bursting into tears. Where was her sweet, placid son? Who had replaced him with this evasive and petulant grunt?

"I'm going to my room"

"You are not. Not until you have told me what you've been up to."

"I told you." He wheeled and his face was a mask of cold hatred. Hatred! Angela recoiled from this face, one she had never seen. Her eyes widened in horror as he glared at her, his voice suddenly slick and menacing. "I haven't done anything."

Angela swallowed hard but stood her ground. "Don't you DARE talk to me in that tone! I'm your mother!"

She was up close to him now, right in his face and his eyes flicked this way and that, focussing first on her left eye and then her right. She held his gaze and waited for a response - one which he seemed to be weighing up. In the end he thought better of it and turned away without saying anything, disgust clear on his face. He headed towards the stairs once more and Angela launched herself forward and grabbed at his left arm.

"Don't you EVER turn your back on me when-"

Tyler wheeled and time slowed to a trickle. Angela watched in shock and disbelief, as his snarling profile twisted towards her over his right shoulder as he pivoted, followed by his arm, extended and swinging in a heavy arc in her direction. She started to lean back, instinctively distancing herself, but her movements were glacial and his arm turned into a hand that loomed towards her. She saw the veins and hairs on it, the bitten nails on his splayed fingers as it filled her vision. And before the pain struck, before the impact made itself felt, Angela watched her lifelong dreams shatter in the back of her son's hand.

"Well, what does Shirley think?" Cullen asked.

"She thinks I shouldn't wash my whites with my colours."

"What?"

"I should wash my whites and colours separately. Apparently." Paul looked bemused. "Some kind of laundry apartheid."

"And you don't think that's a good idea?"

"Nah. Stick 'em all in together. Sink or swim, I say, see what survives. Survival of the fittest innit? Darwin."

Cullen waggled a finger in his ear, trying to dislodge Paul's logic before it took root. "Can we get back to working? I meant what does Shirley think about -"

"Look." Paul leant back, folded his arms and exhaled loudly. "I may not be the sharpest coat in the fridge..."

"Granted."

"But it's like the laundry innit? Darwinian."

"Not for the first time, you have lost me."

"Striving for this, struggling for that. It's like a big

contest, right? And in any contest - EVERY contest - there are winners and losers, yeah?"

"Hence the term *contest.*"

"Exactly! And that's why they call it the rat race. Race, contest, same thing." Paul was gratified to find Cullen was starting to see things his way. "But there are always many more losers than winners. There's usually only one winner, but there's hundreds - thousands, millions - of losers."

"And your point is?"

"Well, statistically speaking then, I am much more likely to be a loser than a winner, aren't I?"

"Perhaps." Cullen said, cagily, reluctant to endorse his friend's fast-approaching conclusion.

"So, why fight it?" Paul shrugged. "Accept your fate with good grace and enjoy what you have. Life's not all bad. Something will turn up. We can't all be Head of the BBC."

"Trust the soup, you mean?"

"Correct." Paul nodded with a smile, his case concluded.

"Drift towards your destiny like... krill." Paul objected to this metaphor but couldn't find a suitable response. Cullen persisted. "Or, take the opposite tack. Throw yourself into your work."

"What?" Paul snorted.

"Work harder. Build a career."

"A career?"

"Alright. Baby steps. But hard work pays off. You could meet your bills, save for a pension-"

Paul cut him off. "Hard work pays off... eventually. In the long run."

"So?"

"Laziness pays off right now! It's a no-brainer."

"Ok, Mr No Brain. If you're not going to work, how are you going to pay your bills?"

Paul scrunched up his features, as if pondering the origins of the universe for the first time. "Well..."

"You're not intending to sponge off Shirley are you?"

"Fuck no!" Paul glared menacingly at Cullen, the very suggestion a wound.

"So...?"

Paul carried on thinking, the silence heavy in the air, until he gave up. "Nope. Got nothing. You?"

"Well, generally if someone needs money they earn it-"

"Next!"

"Or take an income from any savings they have built up."

"Sadly, that train has sailed."

"Or they dispose of any assets they may have."

"Assets?"

"You know. Items of monetary worth."

"Sell something, you mean?"

"It's an idea."

"Would be, if I had anything to sell."

"What about your van?"

"My van? Haven't you been paying attention? My van is knackered. Battery, arse, et cetera. No, wait!" Paul's face lit up, a startling epiphany revealed to him. "It's the soup! Telling me to sell my van."

"The soup?"

"Absolutely!" Paul was triumphant. "How much would you give me for it?"

"Your van?"

"Yeah." Paul prodded. "A grand?"

"I don't want a van."

"£800?"

"You just said it needs a new battery."

"Alright, £750."

"I don't need a van."

"£700?"

Cullen squinted across at Paul and sighed. "Has it got a full service history and a valid MOT?"

"Oh, forget it." Paul stood up, annoyed. "I need a waz." And he disappeared off in the direction of the Gents.

When he came back, Cullen was waiting for him with a strange look on his face.

"What?" Paul asked, senses suddenly alert.

"It's Tuesday tomorrow isn't it?"

"So?"

"So be ready."

"For what?"

"Just be ready." Cullen finished up his glass of water. "How about I give you a tenner to borrow your van for a bit?"

Paul's eyebrows shot up. "How about twenty?"

"How about ten and I'll put a bit of petrol in it."

"It's a diesel."

"And another pint."

Paul ruminated for barely a moment. "You'll need a push to get it going."

FIVE

The padlock was easy this time. Cullen didn't understand it but sometimes that was just how it went. What was it Paul said: *Trust the soup?*

A warm summer breeze whispered over the paddock and brushed his face as he opened the container doors. Despite the fact that it was almost eleven pm, it was barely twilight and perfectly bright enough for him to double-check the instructions on the leaflet from the box. The XC-1100 was simplicity itself, it seemed. Back on the desk where he had found it, Cullen had keenly read the blurb, installed the battery, checked it had some initial charge, and registered it on the wireless network. It was all too straightforward.

Even finding the stuff had been easy.

He had slipped into the warehouse at the rear of the building, parking Paul's van up next to the brewery's own delivery Nissan. In the dusty, tired interior the shiny new camera sitting high in the creaking rafters above the loading bay had winked at him like a co-conspirator. Tracing the wires back from the camera to the server in the small office, he had found the portable camera fresh in its box on the desk, an unopened Christmas present in June.

The soup again.

He stood on a couple of empty crates and planted the camera in the top corner of the container, above the doors, where it would catch any movement inside. He flicked the switch on the back and waved his hand in front of it, watching the light wink on and off again. Satisfied, he locked the container back up and strode back to the van. When Tyler and his crew returned here tomorrow with their haul from The Lamb & Flag, the police would have all the evidence they'd need.

It was only when he was all done and found he couldn't start Paul's van that he was rudely awakened from his soup slumber. But wait a minute. Maybe the delivery van's battery would be compatible.

Just how trustworthy was this soup anyway?

"I'm sorry." Angela's voice was a plaintive, hushed apology. Arthur could barely hear it over the thrum from the photocopier next door.

"Hey, hey hey." He soothed, adopting a hushed tone of his own, and leant forward in his chair. "You've no need to apologise. You've done nothing wrong."

She lifted her head, the heavy veil of hair falling to one side of her face with the tiniest of head movements - unconsciously keen to look good even in her distress - and he could see a huge red weal across her cheek.

"It's happening again." She sobbed and dropped her head, hiding her face once more.

"What is?" Arthur stood up from his chair, newly concerned, and walked around the desk. He sat on the edge next to her forlorn figure and reached out to touch her hands, only to pause and retract. He dug into a pocket instead and offered her his hankie. "Has Tyler hit you before?"

"No!" She hissed, the tears coming again. "Never. I...

I..." She shook her head and broke out crying once more.

Arthur stood aghast at his own inability to do anything apart from show concern while his heart thumped out his anguish as he helplessly looked on. Angela was sitting in his guest chair, her knees clasped together, hands wringing in her lap, head down, sobbing and trying to hide the angry mark on her face from him. From everyone. Like Angela, he was trying his hardest to hold back his own tears. He needed to do something.

Arthur got up, walked round the other side of his desk and knelt down next to her chair. Without further thought, he put his arms round her and rested his head on her shoulder. He didn't know if this made her feel better, but it immediately did wonders for him. "Come on, now." He murmured, trying his best to reassure. "Let's not have tears, hmm?" He looked anxiously up and through his office window, suddenly worried that someone might see them and get the wrong idea.

Or report him to HR.

Wait a minute, he was HR.

Nevertheless, in these post-Weinstein days anything could be taken the wrong way. By an outside observer, for instance. Or by Angela herself. Arthur hastily recollected himself and stiffened, a change in his posture that Angela detected through his hug.

"Is everything ok?" She whispered, softening in his embrace while he tried to hug her tenderly and maintain a rigid formality.

"Yes." He said, honestly. Something about this felt so natural, so lovely, so close. "Don't worry about me. You've had a terrible shock. It's okay to be upset. Normal. Look, take the rest of the day off. Go home. No - don't go home!" He corrected himself, realising that some distance from her son was called for here. "Stay here. You can sit in here. Or lie on the treatment couch in Sick Bay. I can get Patti to bring you a cup of tea." Suddenly he was full of ideas.

"But what about the deliveries? I can't Arthur, I've got a full round to do."

"Shhh. Don't worry about it. I'll ask Freddie to cover. You just take it easy, try and stay calm. You're in shock. We don't want you driving around like this!"

"But-"

"No, but's. That's an order." Arthur pulled his head back from her shoulder and nodded at her mock-sternly. "Ok?"

Angela peeped at him through the tear-damped strands of hair plastered to her forehead. She smiled tearfully. "Ok. Thank you."

"Good." Arthur stood up, instantly all business again. "So, here or Sick Bay - which'll it be?"

She took a deep breath and exhaled loudly and slowly. Arthur wondered if perhaps he had lifted a bigger weight from her than he had realised. "Here, please."

She smiled again, and with that sad face, her eyes all swollen and full, Arthur thought she was the most beautiful, precious thing he'd ever seen. His heart ached in his chest and he swallowed with difficulty. "Right. I'll speak to Freddie and organise some tea for you. You stay right here." He pointed a finger downwards, mustering a gentle authority, then stood to leave.

"Arthur?" Angela lifted her face, revealing the angry mark blooming on her perfect cheek. "Don't say anything to anyone. About this? Please?"

"No. Of course." Arthur took her hand and patted it, revelling in its warmth and softness, and the way her slender fingers looked safely ensconced in his own pudgy palm. And all the time thinking, *what the fuck am I going to tell Freddie?*

"You'll never chuffing guess!" Freddie exploded the moment Arthur walked into his office. "Our light-fingered visitor's only gone and nicked the security camera!"

"What?"

"Left it here last night - on my desk! Come in this morning - there it isn't. Chuff's sake."

"Yes. Ah. Right. Yes. I see." Arthur seemed to be lost in his own thoughts, not taking in the severity of Freddie's news.

"Did you hear what I said, Arthur?"

"Yes, Freddie." Arthur smiled embarrassedly. "Yes, It's just that, well something's... come up. Angela's not well. Nothing serious, you understand. But I need someone to make the deliveries today."

"Nothing serious?"

"No. She's fine. Really."

"So why can't she make the deliveries herself?"

"Because..." Freddie watched Arthur's eyebrows strain upwards. Either they were searching for a convincing explanation to pluck from the ether and insert rudely into this transparent fiction that Arthur was pushing, or they were trying to get as far away as possible from the bullshit he was shovelling out of his mouth. "Because she can't." Arthur pursed his mouth. "It's a confidential Personnel matter, Freddie."

"It's a bollocks matter, is what it is." It was seldom difficult to read Freddie's mind and not often that anyone could mistake him for a cheery soul. This was not one of those times.

"Can you help me out here, Freddie? Please. Just this once."

"Just this once? What do you mean, just this once? I've been wet-nursing her chuffing nipper for a week - her maternal duties, as his Mother. And now you want me to do her chuffing actual duties an' all?"

"Please?"

"Why me?" Freddie crossed his arms and stood his ground. He knew full well how this was going to end, but he was damned if he was going to let Jurassic here walk all over him without due notice that this was not the way of things. He was the Foreman! He had seniority - in fact, come to think about it, he'd been here longer than Arthur! He should outrank this pallid Pilsbury Doughboy, by rights.

"Because I can rely upon you." Arthur smiled again.

"Because you can rely on me!" Freddie repeated, shaking his head. "Of course you can rely on me, I'm your chuffing Foreman! I think that's probably high up on the list of job requirements isn't it? Reliability."

"Freddie. Look." Arthur tried to put two friendly hands on Freddie's shoulders but Freddie stiffened and Arthur stopped midway, presumably thinking better of it. *Point chuffing taken*, thought Freddie. "I wouldn't ask if it wasn't urgent. And important. I can't ask just anybody. It needs someone I can trust. Hmm?"

Freddie snorted. This was bollocks of the highest order and, like a new Rolf Harris album, no-one in their right mind would buy it. But it wasn't so much that Arthur couldn't really trust anyone else to do it, it was more the case that Freddie *knew* that no-one else could be trusted to do it. If it wasn't for him, cracking his Foreman's whip left, right and centre, the whole place would grind to a halt. There'd be salt in the beer and chuffing sand in the barrels and everything would go to shit the minute your back was turned. If Arthur's wet dream was indisposed, for whatever reason, then who else was going to drive the chuffing van? Freddie knew all this, and knew that Arthur knew it and he glared at Arthur, simultaneously suspicious and resentful - like a muddy dog being tricked into having a bath.

"Well?" Arthur prodded.

Freddie exhaled sharply. "Give me the chuffing keys."

He stormed out the back of the warehouse to the loading area where the van was parked, muttering to himself. Chuffing Jurassic, blindly following his dick around, tagging along behind it hoping it would lead him to the promised land. In the meantime he would fall for any sob story - Freddie had heard *all* the rumours, and believed all of them - any Moomin-faced menopausal minger who fluttered their eyelashes or shed a tear or showed a bit of cleavage. Jurassic'd be on them like a randy dog on the nearest leg, panting and jiggling until a cold dose of reality threw him off.

He blipped the alarm off and climbed into the cab.

Now this one, the blessed Angela, who could do no wrong and who Arthur seemed to worship - fair enough, she was a decent looker, Freddie wouldn't kick her out of bed for farting - and she had scrubbed up marvellous for the last Christmas party - but the fact that she went in and out in all the right places and was easy on the eye was no reason to go all doolally, give her a cushy number, and give her chuffing tealeaf scumbag of a son a job as well. Bugger me!

He adjusted the mirrors, checked the manifest sitting

on the passenger seat and punched in the first postcode on the satnav.

And what was wrong now, then? Did she have the painters and decorators in or something? Was that it? Arsenal were playing at home so Muggins here had to man the pumps and drop everything to make sure the customers got their orders? Christ on a bike! One day - one day - he'd be in charge. Then we'd see. Management? Pah! Just tell people what to do, shout at them if they didn't do it quickly enough and fire 'em if they didn't turn up. The rest of your time, just sit on your arse watching it get fat, and count the money as the tills rang. Piece of piss.

Freddie turned the keys in the ignition and for a long moment nothing happened. Then the van coughed, coughed again a little more reluctantly, made an effort to turn over, then gave up.

"You're chuffing kidding me!" He thumped the steering wheel with both hands.

"She's late." Tyler had been checking his watch every fifteen seconds for what seemed like ages already and Tracey sighed impatiently as he did it again. "Definitely late."

"And?"

"And she's never late."

"Never?" Tracey made a face as if to say *she may be your mother but she's not infallible.* Then realised he was sitting behind her so couldn't see it.

"I used to ride with her all the time, remember? She had a sheet with the deliveries on it, in order, and she would pencil times against them all. Made it a kind of game - something to keep me engaged or entertained. See if I could pay attention and challenge her to make it on time."

"Huh" Tracey swizzled her lips and cheeks, trying to scratch her nose without taking her helmet off.

They were both sitting astride the bike, engine off, at the end of the street from The Lamb & Flag. The pub was set back from the road in a small courtyard laid out, optimistically, with tables, chairs and parasols for customers who might want to sit and drink while absorbing the sun's rays for the nanosecond between it rising over the towering rooftops of the solicitor's office on the third floor opposite, and setting behind the church clock tower which clanged out every fifteen minutes and represented the only external sound which could drown out the traffic as it hurtled down the street and out of town.

They were parked at the far end of a row of cars, just before a set of commercial blue waste bins, and had a clear view of the whole road, including the junction with the High Street from which any delivery van would emerge, the road being a one-way street. Opposite the pub was a small row of shops: a newsagent, a florist, a chippie, an estate agents and a bookies. Most of the daily traffic was small cars which would briefly pull up outside the shops, leave their indicators on, while their occupant bought a paper, put a bet on or ordered a quick fish supper, only to depart to the general honking of horns and semi-audible "away with ya" which accompanied any attempt to flout local parking restrictions by other motorists attempting to do the very same thing.

The morning was warm already and Tracey was uncomfortable behind her visor, sweat from her forehead and cheeks soaking gently into the enveloping helmet padding. She lifted her visor and turned round on the bike to half-face Tyler.

"Go in anyway." She urged. "There's no reason to wait for the van."

"There is." Tyler hissed. "It's the plan. The delivery is a distraction. Staff busy loading and unloading, moving crates and barrels. Easier for me to nip in and out."

"Like last time?" She couldn't resist a dig and could almost feel him bristle on the pillion behind her. He flipped his own visor up angrily.

"Last time was... unfortunate."

"Maybe he'll be there again."

"Good." Tyler shrugged, defiantly. "I see no reason why he would be, but if he is - I'll be ready for him." He patted one zipped chest pocket with his left hand and smiled, a devil's smile. Tracey's heart leapt.

"Go on." She whispered, her voice dropping a register to what she hoped was insistent and sexy at the same time. "Why wait? You're good enough. Your plan's good enough." She reached around with her right hand and stroked his thigh, rising up towards his crotch. "No need for any... distraction is there?"

Tyler swallowed audibly, suddenly uncomfortable, and checked his watch again seeming to ignore her caress. He squinted as he surveyed the largely empty street with still no sign of an approaching van.

"Go on!" Tracey's eyes glistened, her hand continuing its wandering, and she bobbed her head slightly upwards in encouragement. "I dare you."

Tyler locked eyes with her for the briefest moment and she saw the blackness in them flare. He flipped his visor decisively down, swung his leg off the bike and strode over the road towards the pub.

"Are you sure you don't need my help?" Paul's voice was almost an uncomprehending whine as he called to Davy through the open cellar door.

"Be fine!" Davy yelled back. "She's late, any road. Maybe she's not coming. Better that you focus on the job in hand right now, mate." He left the rest of the sentence *"And let me keep my kegs undamaged this time."* unsaid.

Paul sighed, disappointed, and bent once more to dip the large brush into the bucket of whitewash. True, he was a bit fed up with joinery; true, he was happy to do a bit of mindless manual labour in exchange for a few pints and a few quid towards a new battery; true, he was never happier than when he was in The Lamb & Flag - except when he was with Shirley, natch. Wouldn't want Shirl to think she came second to the pub. Perish the very thought.

But whitewashing? He couldn't get worked up about it. It had been fine at the start, transforming the dirty, dusty walls to a bright and new white, if not brilliant-white then at least new-improved-off-white-with-a-hint-of-cobweb-white. But the novelty had worn off, mostly because this bending down and dipping his brush then straightening up and painting the walls was playing hell with his back and physical flexibility was not Paul's long suit. Shirley had once asked him what his long suit was and Paul had just grunted evasively and then gone to look it up. Turned out it was something to do with Bridge, the card game, which didn't help. About the only thing Paul knew about Bridge was that it was like sex - if you didn't have a good partner, you needed a good hand.

He smiled at the thought of Shirley, his partner, and their last tangle in the sheets. Temporarily revived by this memory, he looked down at the half-empty bucket and the last wall, only two-thirds done and then sighed again. Maybe if he could finish this off before lunchtime, nip home and catch Shirley on her lunchbreak? Paul smiled at the idea, almost attempting a cheery whistle, and then decided he would crack on and do just that.

After he'd had a quick waz.

Tracey was on high alert the minute Tyler disappeared from view. She started the bike and kept nervously revving the engine, reminding herself she was set to fly the moment he flung himself onto the seat behind her. Her pulse was racing and she felt hot and anxious and excited and horny, all at the same time. This was the high she sought - the excitement and danger and adrenalin of this moment and the one soon to come when Tyler would fly out across the road, she would flip her visor down and, racing with him clinging onto her for dear life, shoot the tight bend at the end of the street and vanish from sight. They would scream and shout with relief and excitement, inaudible inside their helmets, as they rocketed out of town and made their way back to The Cave, where they would hungrily tear at each other's clothes, wrestle themselves half-naked onto the mattress and have hot, thrashing, noisy sex.

Then, when she came down from the high, she'd remember the coke machine and the need to be shut of him.

She flicked her eyes between the open side door to the pub that Tyler had slid in through, and the end of the street for signs of the overdue delivery van. Back and forth, like a metronome, she started to lose herself to the rhythm and began counting the beats as a way of keeping her heart rate under control: pub-one-two-three, van-one-two-three, pub-one-two-three, van-one-two-three.

Hypnotised, it took her a second or two to actually notice that the motorbike engine beneath her had cut out.

Paul was zipping his fly when his phone pinged in his pocket. He took it out and swiped the screen.

INCOMING.

That was all the message said. It was from Cullen.

Christ, what was it with the man? Plans and cryptic messages and shit. Just talk to me, man. Fill me in. I'll understand. He opened the door and stepped out into the corridor, stabbing grumpily at his phone.

Incoming what?

Like a freight train on a collision course, Tyler sprinted around the corner of the corridor as if he was on rails, and then ploughed straight into a large mass moving towards him. His momentum carried him partially over the object, which had collapsed into a pile below him, but still represented a hurdle sufficiently high that he was unable to leap over it. Tyler went down at the second time of asking, the cashbox spraying its contents of silver and notes all across the slippery tiled floor.

When he got to his feet, he still had the knife in his hand and the hurdle had revealed itself to be the crumpled shape of the big bastard who had twatted him with a keg last time. This time he was unarmed and there were no kegs, or anything else for that matter, within reach. Tyler held the knife out threateningly, its blade gleaming in the overhead strip light, and the large man held both his hands up and started backing away towards the double swing-doors.

"Don't do it, kid." The man pleaded. "Not going to end well."

"Oh yeah?" Tyler sneered, pushing forward still as the man continued to retreat. "Why's that then, porky?"

The man was up against the doors now and he backed through them into the cellar and Tyler's hackles rose, the musty memory of this room fresh in his nostrils. The voice of an insistent Tracey rose in his mind to address him:

Get the bastard!

We don't want anything within reach that he can use as a weapon!

Then strike now and get out!

But the clock is ticking - and the cash is gone.

Yeah, again! And this is the guy who denied you. Twice!

But the plan!

The plan's toast. Shank him!

Maybe I can just shut him in and grab some notes off the floor?

It's a swing-door dummy. Cut him - now! And let's go.

The dialogue ricocheted back and forth in his head as he forced the man further into the cellar, his options narrowing with every step. Tyler was just about to win out when his vision suddenly went completely white.

"What the-?" Tracey had looked down at the bike to restart the engine, noticed the key was suddenly missing, and then looked up again. Her outrage was simultaneously extinguished by four things:

1. The delivery van had just appeared at the top of the street.

2. Her ignition key was dangling brightly from a large thumb and forefinger, right in her eyeline.

3. The thumb and forefinger belonged to the man in the cowboy hat they had threatened at The Cave.

4. He was smiling at her.

"Hello again." He said, brightly. "Revving and idling?" He tutted, shaking his head. "Think of the pollution."

"Give me my key back, dickbrain." She said through a clenched jaw, her eyes narrowing.

Neither of these things seemed to make any impression on the tramp. He screwed up his nose and waggled his head from side to side, as if in thought.

"Nah." He said, obviously having arrived at a decision.

Then he launched the key overarm, sending it arcing through the clear blue sky and plopping gaily into the brightly burbling stream which ran along a ditch beyond the edge of the road.

Paul looked on with some satisfaction as the idiot in the motorcycle helmet careered off the cellar walls like a demented pinball. It had obviously dawned on the punk that the thing to do was lift his visor, freshly daubed as it was now with whitewash, but presumably he was reluctant to do this as he realised Paul would then be able to identify him. Whatever, his loss. Paul stood amused at the Keystone Cops effect of this blinded buffoon trying to grapple his way to the exit through the use of touch and memory alone.

Paul reached to dip his brush into the whitewash bucket for a second coat but when he looked up again, somehow the kid had found the exit and was rebounding off the corridor walls following the scent of the outdoors like an injured homing pigeon with a faulty compass.

Chuffing technology, thought Freddie. Chuffing hate it. What's wrong with pen and chuffing paper? Was good enough a few years back. Now they've got to reinvent everything. Can't have a pencil, have to have a stylus. That doesn't work as well as a pencil. Can't have paper, have to have a touchscreen. Which doesn't work as well as paper, can't be seen in the sunlight and needs a chuffing battery!

He stabbed at the now useless satnav, wanting to kill the current job and type in the postcode for the next delivery. Sure, he should probably wait until he'd actually made this delivery, but he was chuffing late! This piece-of-shit van needed three Hail Mary's and a pushstart before it would go and he'd taken to leaving it idling at the last two jobs, hoping it didn't conk out on him while he left it running. And, now he was low on diesel! Bugger me - what else could go wrong?

He grabbed for the manifest with one hand as he steered down the narrow car-lined street with the other. Someone somewhere honked and he hoped for their sake it wasn't at him, or they would get what was coming to them. Just as soon as he'd dropped these chuffing crates off at the... what was it? The Lamb & Flag. At least it was a proper pub name. There was another thing they couldn't bloody leave alone - pub names. Days gone by it was The George, The Prince Of Wales, The Red Lion. Now it was all Three Cockles On The Nightstand, or The Kipper In Short Trousers, or some other chuffing bollocks.

Oh, just wait until he got back to the Brewery and gave Arthur a piece of his mind. He'd think twice about sending him out to do the job his bit of skirt should be doing, by

Christ. It was one chuffing thing after-.

In a heartbeat, Freddie's fuming turned to cold, cold shock as he slammed on the brakes.

It soon occurred to Tyler that, if he was going to escape at all, he had better address his vision problem. This he did by wiping a sleeve across his visor, thereby succeeding in smearing the white mess further and bouncing off the wall again. It was like trying to see out of dirty bathroom porthole while sitting in a one-man bobsleigh.

He lifted his visor which granted some blinkered but clear visibility and took a sharp left towards the bright daylight broadsiding through the open fire-door. As he emerged blinking into the fresh air, clattering through the empty tables and chairs littering the forecourt, his visor slithered stupidly shut again, the whitewash acting as some kind of infuriatingly effective lubricant. He grappled with it, trying to wrestle it free as he half-hurdled, half-ran towards the road and he hoped - because he certainly could no longer see - a waiting Tracey.

Inside his helmet that he swore he would never, ever wear again, Tyler was incandescence itself - a sulphurous flame ignited by a failure to retrieve the money, fuelled by a second defeat at the hands of a bludgeoning loaf and the realisation that he had dropped his knife (again), and fired by a shame that, for all his planning and calculations, he was failing to live up to his own expectations (and, he knew, Tracey's). Only this flame didn't burn with a cool, liquid blue; it burnt with an angry, livid black. As black as his heart, as black his fury, as black as his eyes.

And as black as the radiator grill on the approaching delivery van as Tyler stepped wildly into its path.

SIX

The good weather broke the following week, the June rain returned and the chairs and tables on The Lamb & Flag forecourt stood neglected while inside Paul gulped thirstily at his pint.

"Not bad." Paul, seeing Cullen's expression, slowed his pace and took a sip, trying to nod as appreciatively as a connoisseur - which, in the realm of beer, he supposed, he probably was. "Nutty. Some caramel in there. Aye. Not bad."

"It's called *Pulling Out All The Hops*." Cullen gave a wry smile. "It's alcohol-free."

Paul spat out his mouthful, splattering Ant & Dec at his feet. They barely looked up. "What d'ya give me that for?"

"You said you liked it."

"That was before I knew it wasn't beer."

"It is beer. Alcohol-free beer."

"Contradiction in terms." Paul stated, wiping his mouth with one grubby sleeve, trying to remove the remnants of the taste. "Like vegan sausages. Or American chocolate."

"It's a very popular range, the guy at the bar said."

"With women."

"With non-drinkers."

"Same thing." Sniffed Paul, sitting back, arms folded defiantly at the pint in front of him. "I'm supposed to be celebrating and you give me cat's piss."

"It's alcohol-free beer." Cullen reiterated, as calmly as he could manage. "And what, exactly, are you celebrating?"

"Vanquishing the miscreant." Paul raised an eyebrow proudly.

"Vanquishing the miscreant? You been reading a book again?"

"'Swhat I did."

"By miscreant you mean Tyler McKenna?"

"The very same. Who I twice foiled in his attempts to steal Davy's valuables"

"Does Davy have any valuables?"

"Obv!" Snorted Paul. "Or why would Tyler have been robbing the place? Twice?"

Cullen ignored this circular logic. "And by vanquishing you mean chasing away, so that he fled into the path of an oncoming vehicle?"

"No. I mean obscuring his vision with whitewash from my bucket so that he could be apprehended by the authorities."

"You *have* been reading a book."

Paul ignored him. "Whilst being assaulted."

"You or him?"

"Me! He was going to assault me - again! With a knife - again!"

"Right." Cullen sighed. "Well, beats my plan I suppose."

"Yeah, about that. You could try sharing you know - I'm not a complete bell-end. Incoming." Paul snorted.

"No. You're not."

"So what was the plan then?

"That was my backup plan."

"I was your backup plan?"

"Backup plan to keep you safe." Cullen gave a thin smile.

"Ah, Cullen's got a plan so we're all safe are we? I didn't feel safe with a knife pointing at me."

"Would you have felt safe if you'd known it was part of a plan?"

"Part of a backup plan? That didn't work, you mean?" Paul sniped.

"My first plan was better."

"And what was that?"

"Doesn't matter now, does it?"

"Doesn't it?" Paul was aggrieved. "So you had two plans and you didn't share either of them with me. If I want life to tell me '*bite the pillow, I'm going in dry*' I'll let you know. Maybe next time, a bit more lubrication-"

"That's quite a disturbing mental picture."

"It's a metaphor. Lubrication in this instance is-"

"I get it."

"Yeah, well. You want a plan to succeed, maybe sharing increases its chances - all I'm saying."

Cullen sighed again. "Quite the pub philosopher, aren't you? What with this and the soup."

"Well, its the soup what won it!"

"Hmm." Cullen pondered this for a while. "Tell me more about this soup then."

"You wouldn't understand." Paul smirked. "It's a metaphor."

"Another one."

"What do you want to know about it?"

"Never mind. Cheers." Cullen raised his glass. "To vanquishing the miscreant."

"Aye." Paul scowled at him, not wanting to raise his

own. "And to the magical transformation of my van, now a smoothly-starting miracle machine."

"Really?" Cullen remained impassive.

"Straight up. Since you brought it back, starts like a dream." Paul leaned in close. "What did you do to it?"

"Nothing." Cullen lied. "Must be the soup."

"Eh?"

"The soup that was telling you to sell your van, is now telling you your battery's fine. Get back in the joinery saddle."

"The joinery saddle?"

"It's a metaphor."

"Huh." Paul thoughtfully took a swig from his pint, then put it down swiftly, remembering the contents.

POSTSCRIPT

Tyler McKenna was charged with assaulting his mother, **Angela McKenna**, two counts of attempted armed robbery from The Lamb & Flag, and four other robbery and attempted robbery offences. Tyler did not make a statement, declined to testify at his trial and is now currently in detention at HM Young Offenders Institute Polmont, near Falkirk. As a result of the injuries he received in the road accident he is no longer able to ride a motorbike.

Tracey Marshall was never arrested, since Tyler never made any statements regarding his crimes, and was able to return to The Cave and squirrel away Tyler's motorbike and all other incriminating evidence. She has been spending every evening since the summer searching a ditch for the ignition key.

Angela McKenna fell headlong into the arms of **Arthur Parke** and has barely come up for air since. Finding a man incapable of abusing her made her feel like a new woman and, in the process, released many pent-up desires. Their relationship was consummated on a mattress they found in an abandoned storage container at the rear of the brewery.

Freddie Hughes was subsequently promoted to Brewery

Manager after he diplomatically confronted Arthur with video evidence of his and Angela's liaison in the container. He was, and remains, chuffing delighted.

Arthur "Jurassic" Parke returned the XC-1100 security camera within the agreed four week approval period, free of charge. He has cancelled all memberships of internet-dating sites and has since focussed his romantic attentions on Angela McKenna. He is still waiting on a response from that Nigerian Prince.

"Big" Paul McInnes continues to embellish the story of how he saved The Lamb & Flag. Davy is getting quite sick of hearing it, especially now that Paul finishes it with a lame joke about how Tyler was done for assault but Paul got the battery.

Mungo James Cullen went back to Biggar to scavenge what he could from what was left in The Cave. Amongst his finds were three cans of orange spray paint that he believed he might be able to find a use for, one day.

AUTHOR'S NOTE

My thanks to Broughton Ales Brewery and David McGowan who gave me twelve free bottles of beer. Sorry, I mean a tour of the brewery. For research purposes. Hopefully the punny names I came up with for some of their beers will be useful in any future marketing ventures (perhaps in at least ruling them out as ideas to follow up!) and help offset the fact that I changed the name of the brewery and made up Arthur, Freddie, Angela et al. They bear no resemblance to employees of the brewery, past or present.

I apologise for not featuring other brewery-specific aspects more prominently in the plot, but the delivery van/rider angle was enough I felt. One of the problems with novellas - at least the way I write them - is that they are too short to allow for an intricate comeuppance for the bad guys. In a novel there is room to build a plan and resolve it, taking multiple strands and weaving them tightly together to form a satisfying conclusion to the narrative. In a novella, it's: "Ach, I'm out of pages!"

Thank you to my Beta readers Deidre M, Lynn H, Pete B and John K and Jane - their comments and typo-catching facilities have greatly improved the book you've just finished reading.

Biggest thanks must go, again, to Claire who gave me heaps of constructive feedback and comment on the tone and plot when I foolishly thought it might be finished. The changes I made as a result have hugely improved the final story. You, dear reader, will never know how embarrassed I would be if I had to send each book out in its "alpha" form for you to buy.

Finally, a shout out to the soup. This book is dedicated to it and you, too, could learn to trust the soup.

Or not. It's up to you.

I'm not bothered.

mjf
23.3.2019

Join the Cullen & Big Paul Fan Club!

If you enjoyed the adventures of Cullen and Big Paul, why not join their fan club? You'll get early notice of new books, special offers, a monthly newsletter from the author, unique free content, invitations for discounts and more!

JOIN at **download.markfarrer.com/signup**

Tell others what you thought...

If you enjoyed this book, please leave a review on Amazon

About the Author

You can learn more about Mark Farrer at **www.markfarrer.com** or follow him on Twitter **@mark_farrer.**

Printed in Great Britain
by Amazon

86694632R00068